SURVIVING LOVE

SURVIVING LOVE

A NOVEL

TONDA B. SOLOMON

NEW YORK

LONDON • NASHVILLE • MELBOURNE • VANCOUVER

SURVIVING LOVE
A NOVEL

Published in New York, New York, by Morgan James Publishing. Morgan James is a trademark of Morgan James, LLC. www.MorganJamesPublishing.com

ISBN 978-1-64279-596-7 paperback
ISBN 978-1-64279-597-4 eBook
Library of Congress Control Number: 2019940359

Cover Design by:
Rachel Lopez
www.r2cdesign.com

Interior Design by:
Bonnie Bushman
The Whole Caboodle Graphic Design

Morgan James is a proud partner of Habitat for Humanity Peninsula and Greater Williamsburg. Partners in building since 2006.

Get involved today! Visit
www.MorganJamesBuilds.com

*"If you can learn a simple trick, Scout,
you'll get along a lot better with all kinds of folks.
You never really understand a person until you consider things
from his point of view—until you climb into his skin
and walk around in it."*

Atticus Finch

Chapter One
ALYCE

*A*lyce flipped onto her stomach and propped a large-brimmed hat over her head. In this position, no one could see, just in case she drooled. The umbrella sheltering the wooden chaise on which she lay provided plenty of shade. Her only wish was to drift away into a dreamless nap.

She willed her mind to focus on the lulling sound of the ocean waves, but all she could hear was the little girl from the condo next to hers. What was her name? Chloe, that was it. The family occupied beach chairs two sets down from hers in the long row of bright blue umbrellas. Apparently, it was Chloe's nap time, and she needed it badly. A tug-of-war was going on as the little girl whined, "I don't want to go inside!"

Alyce remembered those days with her own children, all three now grown. Poor little thing. She was cute as a button and loved being on the beach, but Alyce was desperate for peace and quiet and, hopefully, some sleep.

Finally, someone took Chloe inside. Now Alyce was confident she was only minutes away from her own much-needed rest. She found it somehow easier to relax out here with the beach sounds as background noise. Her condo was uncommonly quiet, which allowed her mind to wander to places she preferred not go.

Funny how her attempt to escape the chaos at home had landed her in a place she couldn't rest. She should be relishing this time at the beach. Not a soul needed her to prepare lunch or settle a dispute or braid their hair. Now that the children were older, she could enjoy this trip in a different, more relaxing way.

Maybe it was too much change—an empty house, a vacation alone—but it had seemed like a terrific idea to run away. Alyce and her husband, Michael, had been separated for nine months. His affair had been in full swing for a year and a half. She had found every excuse not to sign the divorce papers, but she had brought them with her and would return with them signed. It merely meant wrapping her mind around being single again, a fact her entire being resisted.

For many who found themselves in her situation, divorce was the epitome of freedom. Who fought for a relationship blighted by infidelity? But her heart and soul had belonged to Michael Keriman for almost thirty years now. She did not want to be free. Even if unwillingly tangled in a giant web of his selfishness and deceit, she saw no easy way to extricate herself.

Not that she loved the person Michael had become. Oh, no. But the smart, charming man of her dreams she'd married? That guy had been her world. And even after she finally knew the truth and he had moved out, she believed he was someone she could wait for, no matter how long it took for him to come to his senses. However, with each day that passed, the likelihood of Michael having some grand revelation seemed more and more improbable.

Now, her aching heart told her she must make a clean break to forge a new path. But her mind—typically levelheaded—spun round in circles, seemingly unwilling to guide one foot in front of the other, much less begin a purposeful march in another direction.

Relaxation would definitely require reprogramming her mind. *Remember, you ran away*, she chided herself. Making a mental note to call her daughter that evening, she closed her eyes.

Alyce wasn't sure how long she slept. She was awakened by something bumping her chair. Pushing up on her elbows, she peeked out from under her cockeyed hat. A Frisbee lay in the sand beside her.

The sun was beginning to lose its strength. What time was it? She flipped her hat aside and stretched her jaw. Man, was she tight. A massage had to be on the agenda for tomorrow. Yawning widely, she rubbed the side of her face and felt the imprint of the rolled towel she had used for a pillow.

Her brain was foggy, but she became aware of two hairy, muscular legs running rapidly toward her. "Hey, sorry about that," the man spoke as he approached. The angle of the umbrella blocked Alyce from seeing his face, but his T-shirt read, "Coconut Joe's."

She maneuvered until she was sitting on the side of the beach chair. "It's fine," she mumbled. She yanked the ponytail holder from her hair and attempted a new one from the mess that tumbled down. Alyce paid him little attention, thinking he would reclaim the disc and return to his game.

She was startled when, rather than just reaching in to grab the Frisbee, he actually ducked his head under the umbrella to retrieve it. He glanced up and stared straight at her with clear, blue eyes. A thick head of sand-colored hair was graying and curly. Alyce noticed how it nicely framed his tan face.

"You reading *To Kill a Mockingbird*?" he asked, squatting down as if to stay awhile. Alyce glanced at the book partially sticking out of her beach bag. The combination of being jolted from a deep sleep coupled with the shock of this disarming person in her space caused Alyce to stammer, "Yes. I mean, well, I mean, of course I've read it before, but that was way back in high school." She paused. "I don't mean *way* back." She shook the cobwebs and spoke succinctly. "It's a classic. I decided I needed to read it again when no one was forcing me. Maybe I'll gain a different appreciation for it." Did that sound snarky?

Hardly able to focus, she decided she must have been solidly asleep. And this stranger was very nice looking. She glanced to see if he was wearing a ring. *Alyce, stop that!* Since when did she check out a man's ring finger? Was it the confusion of sleep? Maybe the tumult of emotions from her impending singleness? *Say something!* she chided herself. "Did someone make you read it in high school?" Inwardly, she groaned at her lack of ability to make small talk.

"I've actually read it several times, just because I wanted to," he said with a smile that revealed perfect teeth. "I did my thesis on Harper Lee for my English major at Alabama. Don't get me started."

Alyce made notes. Cute. Educated. Suddenly remembering her haphazard hair and the fact that her beach hat was laying beside her rather than on her head, she thought, *I must look ridiculous.*

As the stranger talked on about Harper Lee, Alyce attempted to maintain eye contact while inconspicuously reaching for her hat. In doing so, she knocked over the water bottle propped on the top of her bag. They both reached to grab it, and when their hands touched, Alyce felt somewhat bashful like a schoolgirl. Was she now doomed to view everything involving the opposite sex through the lens of "single woman"? She despised Michael in that moment.

Alyce quickly busied herself with the contents of her bag to avoid him seeing her face, where a mixture of embarrassment and awkwardness was causing her to blush. She prayed the usual splotches on her chest weren't making an appearance, too. A feeling she'd not had since high school stirred inside. Was she attracted to him? Deep in the recesses of her psyche a nudge of guilt feebly attempted to make its presence known. Alyce dismissed it. She had nothing to feel guilty about.

"I'm afraid your book might be soggy," he said, holding it up and waving the wet pages in the air. Alyce realized she had no cause for concern. He wouldn't have picked up on her silly emotions. Why should he? He had no idea how empty and hollow she had felt for over a year.

"It's okay. I actually finished it just before I fell asleep."

Alyce never wanted to find herself back in the dating scene. It wasn't fun when she was a teenager, and she had no reason to think it would be better this time, especially at fifty.

A rebellion contrary to Alyce's typically subservient personality stirred inside her. Perhaps that was what shushed the guilt that tried to sound the alarm in her brain. She was processing her emotions when he backed out from under the umbrella and stood upright. He stepped back a few paces so he could see her.

"Are you staying here at Pelican Pointe?" she blurted out. Why didn't she just let him walk away? She wasn't sure, but she felt a strong desire to find out more about this stranger. He continued backward until he was in full view from her perch on the chaise.

"I came in on Friday," he said. He raised his voice as he continued stepping haphazardly in the soft sand. "I'm staying with friends on the third floor. Unit 302."

"That's right above me!" she shouted. Alyce cringed. In that moment, she wondered which would be worse, adjusting to life without Michael or the dreaded awareness of her new marital status. It angered her to be forced into such a quandary, but in light of the zombie-like state she'd been in for months, anger was a good thing.

He laughed as he ran away. "Maybe I'll see you around."

"Maybe," she answered as Coconut Joe turned and ran toward the water and his waiting friends. *Wait, now you've given him a nickname? There's no hope for you, girl. Remember all those friends you walked with through divorces? They were hopeless and distraught until the papers were signed, and then they blew you away when they immediately started dating. Get yourself together!*

Alyce reached for a portion of her towel to fold over her legs. Would she always be self-conscious about her appearance? As quickly as the hint of a flirt had appeared, relaxed Alyce vanished into thin air, replaced by the sad, awkward woman who had arrived just the day before. That woman had come to the beach to process life. Broken and beaten down, she was suddenly weary again and thought maybe she'd best head inside.

Late afternoon had always been her favorite time on the beach, although she rarely had the chance to enjoy it. Her husband preferred dinners out whenever they vacationed. She was happy to cook or order pizza so they could linger, but Michael always chose the lines at the restaurants, forcing her to abandon her chair early to ready herself and the children for dinner.

Over the years, Alyce had gradually adopted a beach style of minimal makeup and a ponytail. Fortunately, she was attractive and able to pull it off. Besides, she loved for her girls to shine, and making sure they were the prettiest left little time for herself. Alyce had to admit she wished occasionally to get dolled up in a cute dress and heels, even if it was at the beach. Who knew if there would ever be a reason to do that again?

She wasn't sure why she favored the beach in late afternoon, but the tranquility of the ocean at that time of day was particularly appealing, forever strong and sure and faithful with its recurring rhythm of waves. And as evening glided in, almost unnoticed, the sun danced differently upon the water, and fewer people crowded the air with their noise.

With resolve, Alyce forced herself to lean back in her chair and stay. She could learn a new life, though it would take time. To begin, she could allow herself to follow a different routine while at the beach, starting with staying right where she was until the sun had set. Besides, she had a Frisbee game to enjoy.

~~~~~~~~

When Alyce finally went inside, she found she was sleepy and contemplated showering and going to bed. She wasn't yet ready to brave dinner alone, even though she had noticed a great little beachside cabana where the burgers smelled delicious and an outdoor restaurant with a menu board that advertised fresh red snapper with a kale and quinoa salad. "Maybe tomorrow night," she told herself.

Alyce was thankful she finally had an appetite for real food after weeks of poor eating. She wished she was one of those women who never ate when they were heartbroken, but sadly, she chose to eat her sorrow away. She could finish half of a pound bag of peanut M&Ms before she even realized she was feeding misery with misery. Often, she stopped for a hot caramel sundae at Sonic on the way home from her daughter's house at night. Not a great choice, even if it was all she ate in a day.

She eyed the deep tub in the bathroom and a wild idea crossed her mind. How long had it been since she had soaked in a hot bath? She could light some candles and maybe turn on some quiet music. No agenda and no interruptions—a grand idea.

As water ran into the tub, she added a few drops of lavender for relaxation and some baby oil to soften her skin. Alyce wrapped her hair in a towel, then slipped under the warmth of the water. Admittedly, she liked the temperature exceptionally hot, and this bath did not disappoint. At first, her body tensed against the extreme heat, then slowly relaxed as tension oozed from her like the hot caramel running down her sundae. She smelled the coconut sunscreen mingling with the lavender, not at all unpleasant.

Once she was cocooned in her liquid therapy, she allowed her mind to revisit the encounter with Coconut Joe on the beach. *Will I even bother to date?* she wondered. Again, she felt oddly bashful when she recalled his wave as he left the beach with his friends. Was it her imagination, or did he go slightly out of his way to pass close by so he could yell, "See you tomorrow!" It had to be coincidence.

She frowned a little and scolded herself for thinking negatively. Why wouldn't he want to be friendly? She was very attractive for her age, at least on her better days, though no man had actually told her she was beautiful in quite a long time.

That led her thoughts toward an all-too-familiar path of sadness where she took several steps before turning her thoughts around by saying her latest scripture prayer: "Lord, will You take every one of my thoughts captive to Your glory and Your honor? I know I am Yours, and You make me valuable, even priceless. Whatever is true, honorable, just, pure, lovely, commendable—if there is anything worth praise—I choose to set up camp on those things. There is no fear in love, but perfect love casts out fear."

She hummed a favorite hymn she'd known since her teenage years. When she reached the chorus, she sang softly as tears slid down her cheeks and plopped into the water around her, *Turn your eyes upon Jesus. Look full in His wonderful face. And the things of earth will grow strangely dim, in the light of His glory and grace.*

Leaning back, she closed her eyes and imagined God plucking the horrid thoughts from her mind like weeds. All He left behind were vibrant flowers that represented the good that had come from her twenty-six-year marriage. Her two sweet girls, Maggie and Lillian, and delightful son, Harrison, swayed freely in her garden.

Two days before Alyce had left for the beach, Maggie and her husband, Jackson, brought over a basket of goodies for her trip, along with the joyous news that she was going to be a grandmother. Alyce had only seven months to prepare. She imagined a lovely cluster of daisies signifying that innocent new life.

She marveled that her chatty Maggie had kept this secret for as long as she had. It seemed she and Jackson had only just married, but much had changed in two years. The memory of Maggie and Jackson's wedding swayed softly in her garden.

Alyce focused on the good things in the past and the tranquility of this present moment. She would not allow her mind to venture to the future. Her vision blurred when she tried to think forward. It was just as well. Worry, doubt, and the unknown lived there. Whenever she tried to "go there," she imagined Jesus stepping in front of her. The words, "Look full in his wonderful face," reminded her that she must remain fixed on him to maintain her sanity. She inhaled the aroma of the lavender and coconut and relaxed.

When the water cooled and her fingers and toes resembled raisins, Alyce stepped from the tub. Careful not to slip in the baby oil that lingered as the water drained, she patted herself dry and studied her faint tan lines. She slathered on her favorite lotion, with no one to comment about the smell as Michael sometimes would. It had always been delightful to her. She shimmied into brand new pajamas she'd bought to treat herself. To say she was relaxed did not do justice to the mellifluous mood Alyce found herself in.

She padded into the living room to the comfy chair and ottoman by the balcony door, where she'd deposited her Bible, her journal, and the two latest books she was reading. With so many titles on her list, she had a lot of catching up to do.

With a view of the ocean and sky, she had an ideal spot to spend time with the LORD. The edge of eternity stretched before her: the sun on the water by day and the moon by night.

Alyce slid open the door to receive the full orchestration of the nighttime concert the ocean offered. The roar of the deep seemed louder at night. She liked thinking God turned up the volume to remind her that in the darkest places of life, His grace was greater. She called this beautiful arrangement *I AM*, written and arranged and conducted by Creator God. Standing in the doorway, the music washed over her with the warmth of the breeze, and she sensed His invitation to sit a while.

Alyce tucked her feet underneath and cozied into the chair. She whispered, "Thank You," suddenly keenly aware of the blessing and comfort of where she was. How incredible to be in that place at that time, a respite and a refuge for her weary soul. She had brought such a burden with her. The magnitude of her gratitude caused her to close her eyes and simply be still. There were no words, just a heart of praise.

Alyce wasn't sure how long she sat. The banter of a group of kids passing on the beach below jolted her from her reverie. She picked up her Bible and journal and spread them before her on the ottoman.

Journaling was new for her. Never short on words, Alyce had learned the value of writing out her feelings. Now she kept a journal of her prayers, her most intimate and personal conversations with her heavenly Father. Journaling had made Him more real to her in recent months than ever before. Whatever she wrote on those pages was safe with Him. There she gave voice to her darkest fears, truest desires, and deepest hurts, all laid before the one who made her and knew her well.

She opened her journal and began with praise. She hadn't always done that but learned during a study of the Lord's Prayer how effective praise was in centering her thoughts. She found it made her prayers bigger and bolder to acknowledge His holiness and His power before anything else. So, she began with praise.

Sometimes the words to a song would flow from her pen. More often, random thoughts to describe Him would flood her mind, and she would write them as a greeting. She felt silly at first, but then it became a challenge to think of new and different words to describe Him.

One day she was journaling and realized this was similar to the way she'd greeted her kids in the mornings when they were growing up. They would wander into the kitchen for breakfast, and she'd greet them with many different names.

"Morning, Sunshine!"

"Hello, Captain Amazing!"

"Welcome to Monday, your Majesty!"

She was now doing this with the King of the Universe, and it gave her so much joy to think of new ways to acknowledge His presence.

Alyce felt a little thrill to think that soon she would be doing something similar for her grandchild—another cause for praise. She knew just how to open her journal entry on this evening. "Greetings, Giver of 'Grand' Life!" she scribbled in her journal.

Then she moved on to confession. When she'd first started journaling, this part was hard for her. She wasn't a thief or a murderer. She didn't habitually lie, and she certainly wasn't the adulterer. One in the family was more than enough, and he was quite adept.

But that declaration led her to something more sinister. She was prideful. She had to admit that she could be pretty smug at times about all she *hadn't* done. Truth was, she had been unfaithful to the Most Faithful, and it wasn't a one-time thing. When she acknowledged her pride, it opened her eyes to more ways she had sinned beyond violating a simple list of commandments.

Alyce laid down her pen and leaned back into the chair. Her thoughts drifted to her husband. She wondered where Michael was at that moment and what he was doing. She breathed a simple prayer of protection for him and that God would guard his heart and mind in Christ Jesus. She'd done that many times since he had left their home. How long would those prayers continue? Even after the divorce was final? Alyce drew in a deep breath and smiled a little as the trace smell of coconut and lavender teased. In her spirit, something whispered, "Child, everything is going to be okay."

Chapter Two

MICHAEL

*M*ichael loved the fuss he created when he arrived at his favorite
restaurant. The shiny, black sports car was a valet magnet,
and two young men in red vests raced toward him as he pulled to the
curb. Handing over the keys, he stepped into the slightly darker interior
of the restaurant and allowed his eyes a moment to adjust as he scanned
the tables.

He spotted her, sitting in his usual booth. She was much younger
than he and a little too eager, waving to him like a schoolgirl across
a playground. He rushed over in hopes to squelch the enthusiasm
before it drew attention. He struggled with how to explain his new life
if challenged, but his uncertainty was juxtaposed with indignance; he
owed no one an explanation for his actions.

Michael had specifically instructed the hostess to never seat him in that booth. Although the best in the house, he and Alyce had spent too many evenings there together. Michael didn't like the reminder of her.

He would have stopped coming to this restaurant altogether, but his ego loved the notoriety of being "known" by staff and wouldn't sacrifice the prestige of instant seating when others waited weeks for a reservation. Besides, the food was incomparable, and he was eating out a lot these days.

The corner booth was a semicircle that faced outward into the restaurant. Michael liked being able to see everyone. No surprises if a friend or client approached his table. It also lent him an air of celebrity, if only in his imagination. Michael was highly successful, and he liked to think everyone knew it. Whenever he ate there, he was certain others noticed the preferential treatment he received. But there were memories attached to it, too. He didn't like to admit that it bothered him to sit in "their booth," but it did.

When the owner came around, as usual, to chat, he would remind him that he had requested no longer to be seated there. As he slid into the booth, Michael could have sworn he smelled that crazy lotion Alyce always wore. He liked to complain about it, but in that moment, he found it absurdly nostalgic. *Must be my imagination,* he mused.

He looked over at Cassidy, the motivation for stepping out of his marriage and into his dreams of a more exciting life. He relished the memory of Alyce's angry smirk when she found out the name of her nemesis.

Though out of character for her, she shrieked, "Cassidy? Seriously? Isn't that a stripper's name? Or, actually worse, I think that's the name of one of Harrison's friends!" Harrison was their nineteen-year-old son, and the dig about her age was not lost on him. Michael didn't actually know for certain—and really didn't care—how old Cassidy was. She was captivated by him and made him feel something Alyce hadn't in quite some time.

She was beautiful and seemed to be smart, too. She scooted closer to him and gave him a long, welcoming look from her big, brown eyes. She had come from work but had removed her suit jacket and strategically unbuttoned the top button, giving him a hint of lace underneath. He never remembered Alyce wearing anything with lace. She was only straight-laced and buttoned up all the time. *Prim* and *proper* were adjectives Michael would use for his wife.

Michael shook his head. Why in the world was he thinking about Alyce? That had been happening more frequently, and it had to stop. It ruined his day, her barging into his thoughts unwelcome and unbidden. He motioned to their server, who hurried over with Michael's standard gin mule and asked, "Shall we begin with the usual appetizer, sir?" Michael took a sip and nodded his approval. Then he motioned the server back with the flourish of his hand and said, "Wait a minute. Let's change it up a bit tonight."

Wasn't that why he and Alyce had drifted apart? Everything was just "the usual"? Michael was growing angry. She was ruining everything, and she wasn't even there.

"Let me see a menu."

As the server stepped away, Michael looked up to see his and Alyce's friends Allen and Kristen Jozwik approaching the table. Michael had only seen Allen once since he'd moved out of the house, and he hadn't seen Kristen at all before now. He braced himself for the awkwardness he felt certain was coming.

Michael and Alyce had shared evenings out with Allen and Kristen, and this initial encounter was going to be difficult. They had raised their kids together at church, the baseball field, and dance recitals. This was one of those moments for which he had rehearsed countless times.

To his surprise, both Allen and Kristen spoke warmly. He was floored when Kristen extended her hand to Cassidy and introduced herself. He noticed she did seem to have an odd stare, but who would blame her? Women were protective of each other, and Kristen would definitely be on the defense in Alyce's stead. This warm greeting, however, wasn't the response he expected. Maybe transitioning wouldn't be so hard after all, sort of like changing a tire.

Even Michael flinched at that thought. *Whoa, buddy! Surely you're not that crass.* As quickly as the thought arrived, it disappeared. Michael's flagrant ego allowed no room for abasement. This was something he'd been dreaming of his whole life: a thriving legal practice, a fine sports car, and a beautiful girl on his arm. What guy didn't long for that? Too bad Alyce had to be cut out of the picture.

His reverie was broken when he heard Kristen say, "It's nice you guys could have a business dinner while Alyce is at the beach. I wondered how you were faring all alone, Michael."

So that explained Kristen's hospitality toward Cassidy. She assumed she was a business associate. Hadn't Alyce told Kristen anything at all about their separation? He had moved out nine months prior. He assumed that Alyce had let friends know of their pending divorce by this point. He did not want to be the one to do the deed and certainly not here under these circumstances.

With no time to ponder that thought, he felt, rather than saw, Cassidy's raised eyebrow and piercing gaze. She awaited his explanation as to who exactly she was.

"Cassidy is one of my junior associates at the firm." Michael smiled rather largely while looking back and forth between Allen and Kristen's faces. He chose to ignore Cassidy's face, but the kick under the table was unavoidable.

Suddenly aware of the heat rising in his cheeks—and even more aware that she was sitting awfully close for an associate—he shifted uncomfortably. This was not going as he had anticipated. He was prepared for a cool exchange with their friends. He did not expect to be the one to break the news that his marriage was over and had been for some time.

Kristen seemed to be cluing in because her gaze hardened slightly.

"I'm happy that Alyce has taken time for herself at the beach. She does so much for others. I'm sure she's getting ready for that new grandbaby."

Grandbaby? Michael's thought screamed.

He was instantly furious. He knew nothing about a grandbaby, but he would never let them know that. The kids were angry and upset over their parents' separation, but to not tell him about his first grandchild? This was absurd. He was going to excuse himself the minute they left and get to the bottom of this.

Maintaining his composure, Michael realized that he didn't even know Alyce was at the beach. How dare they all make plans and keep secrets behind his back? The irony of that thought passed right by him. He was too self-absorbed, and all his energy was focused on keeping his cool. He was in charge, and he would survive this encounter.

"There certainly are a lot of changes going on around the Keriman household," Michael said as he nodded and put on his best lawyer smile. *Gotta keep it together, Michael.* Thankfully, Kristen and Allen's server appeared and asked if she could start some drinks for them. They took the cue and headed toward their table.

"Let's have lunch soon," Allen turned back and casually said. "It's been too long."

I bet you'd like that, Michael thought. "Sure thing," he smiled and lied. He had no intention of having lunch with and getting drilled by someone who would never understand, let alone approve, of his decisions.

As soon as they were safely out of distance, Michael grabbed his phone and searched the call history. To his amazement, he saw three missed calls from Maggie and one from Lillian, all from the evening before and roughly within the span of a half hour. How had he missed these? Michael scooted quickly out of the booth and tossed Cassidy a quick, "Be right back."

Before she could respond, he was walking away and dialing Maggie. He threaded his way through the tables and noticed another friend at a table in the corner. He nodded a greeting as he backed through the side door that led to a small patio. No one would be seated out there, as spring was still too cool for outdoor dining in Nashville. He found a chair as he waited for Maggie to answer her phone. He hung up and dialed it again, willing her to answer.

When nothing came of his attempts, he called Lillian instead. She picked up on the second ring, but before he could even begin, she launched her own tirade.

"Where have you been?" she demanded. "And why wouldn't you take Maggie's calls?"

She drew in a breath, considering all she wanted to say, but made herself stop. Not expecting such a response, he hastily decided to take a different approach. He loved his children and could not afford to exasperate them more than he already had. They were squarely on Alyce's team these days.

"Hello to you, too!" he replied as lightheartedly as possible.

With a pause on the other end, Lillian seemed to gather herself. "Hello, Father," she finally said tritely. That was it. No "how are you" or "what's going on" in Lillian's typically chipper voice. And what was up with *Father*? What happened to *Dad* or, better yet, *Daddy*?

Michael softened his tone, took a deep breath, and began again. "Hey, Lilli-girl," using his pet name for her since she was a baby.

"Apparently a lot has been happening, and I've been AWOL. I tried to call Maggie, but she didn't answer. What's going on with everyone?" Lillian's voice showed little emotion.

"Maggie needs to tell you something very important, and you wouldn't take her call."

"I don't know how I missed it!" he said. "I was at home all last night and just now saw that I missed calls from you both."

"She left a voicemail," was the only response he got.

Michael had left his glasses on the table, so he held his phone at arm's length and squinted to see the screen. A tiny number in a red circle indicated he had a message to which he'd not listened. This was totally uncharacteristic of him.

He felt a twinge of anxiety as he noted how Alyce had always been his connection to the kids, keeping him informed of what they were up to. This was especially true since they'd all left home for college and beyond. He would have to up his game because his kids were his world. When did life get so complicated?

"I see you're right," Michael replied calmly. "I will try her again and leave my own voicemail. And how have you been?"

"Daddy, where are you?" came the reply. He sensed a quiver in Lillian's voice as he searched his mind to try and recall anything particular that was going on. His instincts were telling him he was supposed to remember something, but for the life of him, he couldn't recall it. Mild panic ensued as he suddenly wondered if he was supposed to be somewhere.

"I was grabbing a little dinner. What are you up to?" he queried, silently praying that the answer would be simple and not involve anything he should be doing right at that moment.

He heard Lillian taking a deep breath and could visualize her pushing her tongue between her teeth and her front lip in an effort to control her tears. She'd learned that from her mother. For some reason, it was cute when Lillian did it but had become annoying in Alyce.

"I'm at the school," came the reply. "I've been in the studio for twelve hours trying to get the rest of the photos ready for my show." That was it! Lillian was an art major at Belmont. Her senior exhibit was coming up. What was that date?

"You sound exhausted," Michael soothed. "Have you been eating?"

"I had a stale bagel around eleven, and I've been drinking coffee all day." Lillian sniffed. Michael smiled as he pictured his grown little girl twirling a piece of her hair as she always did when she was tired. "I think I saw some leftover pizza in the fridge. I can eat that when I get back to the apartment."

"Well, you'd better take care of my girl. I'd hate for her to miss her own show." He winced as he then asked, "And what is the date for that again?"

"Dad!"

"What? I'm not looking at my calendar," he fibbed again. He had been doing far too much of that lately. Dishonesty wasn't a character quality he tolerated in others. Funny how adept at it he'd become.

"It is May twenty-third at the Schoenberg Gallery," Lillian announced. "I hope you can come for the evening. It begins at seven."

"I would not miss it, even if they'd just pulled all of my teeth!"

"Ewww, Daddy, why do you have to say something like that?" Lillian giggled in spite of herself. Then she remembered she was supposed to be angry and played it cool. "Please do call Maggie right away."

Michael missed his time with his girls. They had always been his universe until they did what all children do and had to grow up. He was still figuring out how to balance so much change.

"I love you, Lilli-girl. I'll talk to you soon."

"Love you, Daddy. Bye now."

Michael made one last attempt to reach Maggie before heading back inside. Still no answer. He rubbed his hands together to warm them. Though chilly on the patio, he imagined it was nothing compared to the chill he would encounter at the table with Cassidy. Making his way back across the restaurant, he realized she wasn't sitting where he'd left her. He glanced around the room, making eye contact with Allen and Kristen, who were watching him. Once in the booth, he looked back at his phone to check voicemails. Sure enough, Maggie had left one last night at 8:27 p.m.

"Hey, Dad. I have a bit of news to share with you and wondered if we could have lunch tomorrow. Guess you're busy right now. I really need to talk to you. I tried to call a couple of times. Hope you're doing well. I miss you." A pause. "Anyway, call me when you can."

As Michael listened to the voicemail a second time, he watched Cassidy make her way across the restaurant. She was certainly a beautiful young woman, but at that moment, something in Michael's spirit felt very old. He was tired and not at all feeling like the successful guy in the Maserati who arrived just thirty minutes before.

Was it his imagination, or did she not seem quite as upset as he thought she would? She slid around to get cozier with him, but he caught himself keeping a distance. Whatever made Michael feel invincible, as if he answered to no one, had gone out the window. He didn't dare look around. Suddenly he felt that all eyes were on them—not a good thing.

"Is everything okay?"

Cassidy coyly slid her toe up his leg. He *wanted* it to make him feel good, but at that moment, it did nothing.

"Yeah, I just missed several calls from my girls last night. That's odd because I was right there the entire time."

Cassidy leaned in and purred, "Except when you took that long shower. You had a couple of calls from Maggie, but I sent them to voicemail."

Michael had had enough for one day. How dare she intercept calls from his daughters? The evening was ruined. He tossed her a hundred-dollar bill. "Enjoy your meal. I'm out. See you at the apartment." He didn't slow down, and he didn't look back.

"Leaving so soon, sir?" the valet asked.

"There's an extra fifty for you if my car is here in less than a minute."

He turned to look the valet in the eye, but he was gone, heading off to retrieve one black Maserati.

Michael planned to drive around a bit to clear his head. He tried Maggie again and left a voicemail this time. His stomach growled, reminding him that he had worked through lunch and had only a protein shake for breakfast. He was honestly starving. He had a brilliant idea.

~~~~~~~~~~

Lillian looked up from her laptop. She was perched behind a long table in the art building. The table was one of three that formed a U-shape with stools lining the outside. The low-slung fluorescent lights above the tables didn't seem to provide enough illumination to reach the corners of the large room, making it appear dark. Partially sculpted lumps of clay, easels with canvases and paints strewn about, and other evidences of promising genius made a creative trail around the room. A few other students worked diligently on projects of their own, oblivious to whatever was transpiring around them.

It took her a second to recognize the striking older gentleman walking across the room carrying a pizza box and two giant drinks from her favorite place with the crushed ice. He stopped directly in front of her. Lillian looked up into a familiar face that was also someone she hardly recognized anymore. He sat one of the drinks beside her with a look so weary she melted.

"Hello, Daddy."

Chapter Three
ALYCE

*A*lyce woke with a start. Where was she? Her wide eyes darted furtively, scanning the darkened room. A hint of the brilliant sun on the ocean tried to peek around the edges of the blackout drapes, reminding her where she was. Alyce relaxed. She was in a safe place, but the sadness she'd hoped to leave at home had travelled with her, concealing itself until she was alone. Now it pulled its disguise and wrecked her with its rude intrusion.

Her thoughts drifted to their bedroom at home—*her* bedroom at home. She had dressed it with only minimal window coverings because the view was so lovely. Large windows framed scenes of a tranquil wood, ever changing with each passing season. Alyce loved the beach, but she adored her woods. The beach made her feel relaxed and unscheduled. Her woods made her feel safe and nurtured her soul.

She thought of the memories tucked all around the homeplace, from the mailbox at the curb with its creeping Mandevilla to the old tire swing on the tree out back. Alyce had fallen in love the first time she'd seen their home. Yes, she could say that. *Their* home. It had been their home for over twenty years, since right around the time they'd discovered their second baby, Lillian, was on the way.

She wondered if she'd be able to continue living there. From the minute Alyce had confronted Michael and he'd actually been honest about his affair, he'd said he didn't want her to worry about a thing. He would take care of her. But then, he'd always taken *care* of her, yet there had been plenty for which she should have been concerned.

Alyce's heart literally ached at knowing he had taken this girl, this Cassidy, there on occasions when she and the children had gone to visit her parents in Alabama. She wondered if other women had come into her home uninvited. Women who had slept with *her* husband in *her* bed.

Michael had assured her Cassidy was the only one. Why should she even believe that? Why should she ever believe anything from him?

When Michael told her about his desire to move to Nashville not long after they were married, she was reticent. Alyce had lived all of her life in their small town in Alabama, and it had never crossed her mind that she might one day leave. She came from a middle-class family. Alyce was pretty, but not like the attorney's wives she'd met at the firm when Michael interviewed. The partners had hosted a dinner party for the potential recruits and their spouses. Alyce wore a simple blue dress and the pearls Michael had given her at their wedding. But these women were glamorous. They'd been fluffed and plumped and surely had stylists.

That was not Alyce's way. Her mother had raised her to present her best self, always wear lipstick, and never put on airs. A woman should be known more for her actions than the reaction she could elicit. Pretty is as pretty does was not merely a saying at her house. It was a mantra. Alyce purposed early on that her greatest achievements would come through the success of her husband and children. As bizarre as it sounded, this was a way of life she had embraced. Her turn would come.

Maggie was not yet born at the time they moved, so they decided to rent a small place. This provided a chance to learn their way around Nashville before choosing a neighborhood. Their two-bedroom bungalow had proven a great starter as Michael progressed in the firm and Alyce worked at Vanderbilt in the office of the provost. When Maggie came along, her nursery was tiny, but life was serene.

Alyce first eyed their home quite by accident one day when she encountered traffic issues on her way to an appointment with the pediatrician. Maggie hated her car seat and was screaming, so Alyce opted to try the side streets to avoid the congestion. In her haste, she'd missed a turn and ended up passing the beautiful old home. She had no idea where she was, but she remembered exactly how she felt driving past. Had she not been in a hurry with a hysterical child in the backseat, she would have turned around and gone back to write down an address.

In the following weeks, Alyce turned down every side street in the area, attempting to locate the house until, at last, she found it. She was careful to drive by at least once a month or more, just in case the house went on the market. She didn't dream they could afford such a place, but she always checked. It surprised her how calm Maggie would get when she drove onto the street. Her jibber jabber would become lively, and she would rattle off strings of happy nonsense. Alyce took it as a sign. Of what, she wasn't sure, but surely some connection existed between the house and how it made them both feel.

After a year of driving past, the day finally arrived when she turned the corner and saw a *for sale* sign. Alyce's heart skipped a beat. The house appeared empty, so she turned in the driveway, imagining what it might be like if it were hers.

Maggie was sleeping peacefully in her car seat, so Alyce lingered toward the end of the drive. She imagined what the interior might look like and how she would decorate if it were hers. She could imagine the front door dressed at Christmas and the lights from their tree twinkling in the window. Maybe she'd find space for her grandmother's grand piano, currently in storage.

It appeared to be an ideal house, all the way to the very back of the garden. The backyard was perfect for Maggie and the new life now growing inside her. Though frivolous, after that day, Alyce turned around in the drive on a regular basis. She figured it wasn't hurting a soul. Each time, she got a little bolder, inching farther down the long driveway that led to the beautiful house on the edge of the woods.

One crisp fall day, Alyce got up her nerve to get out and look in the windows. She and Maggie had a full morning of errands, and the poor thing had fallen asleep just as Alyce was ready to head home. She figured it would be a good idea to let Maggie sleep while she stole a look for herself.

The minute she turned the corner, an ominous feeling rose up. Something had changed. It took her a second to realize the sign had changed. SALE PENDING. She could have turned in one last time and still looked in the windows, but suddenly she felt silly for her dream of owning such a place. She drove home and told Michael that "their house" had been sold. Michael seemed genuinely sorry, even though he had only seen it once. He knew that Alyce longed to make it their own.

"How do you know you'd even like the inside?" he'd asked. "It may be old and outdated for all you know."

"It wouldn't matter," Alyce sighed. "I think it would have been perfect, or I could have made it that way for us."

The weekend came, and Michael and Alyce set out with Maggie in tow for their Saturday fun day. Michael asked Alyce to look for his sunglasses in the unusually messy glove compartment. He knew her well, for she began cleaning and organizing the space, oblivious to where they were going.

"I don't see your glasses in here, but how do you find anything? I've never seen this space so messy! What does this key go to?" she asked, holding a shiny new key on a Welcome Home Realty keychain.

"Maybe it goes to this door," Michael said, and suddenly Alyce realized that they had turned into "her" driveway. They drove to the end of the front sidewalk as if they owned the place. "Why don't you give it a try?"

Alyce stared at Michael for only a moment, then bounded from the vehicle, key in hand. She shook as she approached the front door. The key fit the lock on the first try. Before she could open the door, Alyce turned to call Michael to join her, but he was already there by her side, holding Maggie. What a priceless memory of a thoughtful, generous gift that took much care in planning.

Alyce shook violently, casting the memory aside. A rush of emotion unlocked inside of her, and she wept bitterly. She sat up in the big, empty bed and hugged her knees to her chest, hardly able to breathe.

Why, Michael? Why, oh, why, oh, why?

With nothing she wouldn't have done for him, she had loved her husband fiercely—yet it wasn't enough. *She* wasn't enough. All of life's experiences that had led up to now were priceless treasures she kept safely in her memory bank. Treasures she had thought they both shared and would unpack together in days to come when they were missing their house full of children and remembering their youth.

But she had been put in her place. For Michael, her memories represented a long list of times she didn't realize he was unhappy. He had said this to her on that dreadful day when she finally confronted him with proof of what she had known in her heart. He had not been happy for a *long time.* Those were his very words. Their life was boring, and she just didn't excite him. He had given a grand performance because he had seemed in love with their life and their family. Even with her.

"You haven't been happy with us since you met *her*!" Alyce screamed out loud into the darkness as tears streamed down her face. "This is not my doing! You...*you* decided to look other places, and now you've found something else that isn't true or real. You've traded everything we built for a lie! You are a fool, Michael Keriman. A stupid, selfish pig of an idiot! And I hate you!"

It felt so good to say it. *I hate you!*

Alyce screamed it over and over, each time dulling the ache in her chest. She knew it wasn't true. She didn't hate Michael, but she hated who he had become. She hated how he was behaving and what he was doing to their family.

Her heart hurt for her babies. Sure, they were grown, but their entire foundation had been shaken, and she prayed every day that they would not forget the good times. That they would love their daddy no matter what. That they would be quick to forgive, even as they saw what the entire situation was doing to their mother.

Alyce thought she heard a tap at the door. She was horrified at the thought of someone seeing her like this. Wiping her tears, she hopped out of bed and raced through the living room to peek through the peephole. Who would be at her door? Her foot brushed against a piece of paper lying on the floor as she stood on her toes and placed her eye against the tiny hole. She scanned the distorted horizon, but not a soul was in sight.

Grateful for any distraction, Alyce accepted it as an interruption to end her tirade. She despised the extreme outbursts. She'd had quite a few of them lately, stemming from her frustrated attempts to express so many foreign emotions. Each "episode" meant conceding emotional ground to Michael, allowing him control of her feelings. *Who is the fool now?* she chided herself.

Time to welcome the day, she pulled on the drapery cord and recoiled as the room filled with sunshine reflecting off the water, which was as blue as Alyce had seen it. She made her way into the kitchen and pulled out a K-cup to make her coffee.

On the weekends, she and Michael had always indulged in a full pot of coffee, rather than making a single cup at a time as they did on weekdays. They would share the newspaper and drink as many cups as they liked as they enjoyed the leisurely comfort between them. Alyce bordered on morose as her mind instinctively reacted, *I guess I'll never enjoy a lazy morning in my PJs with an entire pot of coffee again.*

She snapped at herself, *You are crazy!* Rolling her eyes at her own dramatic response, she spoke sternly to herself, *You can brew a pot of coffee whenever you darn well please and pour the leftover down the drain! Or drink the entire pot if you'd like!*

She defiantly pulled out a filter, filled the carafe with water, and set about making a pot of coffee. Before long, the heady aroma filled the room, and Alyce was settling into her chair with a piping hot cup. She noticed a few folks walking on the beach, but it was still early for most. A tractor had recently come along and made neat rows in the sand as it raked and sifted through the previous day's chaos. Alyce picked up the book she'd left open facedown on the ottoman the night before and scanned the page to remember where she'd left off.

Suddenly, she realized she'd never even looked at the piece of paper she'd stepped on. Where was it? She couldn't remember picking it up, or did she? Perhaps she'd absentmindedly tossed it into the trash. Alyce lifted the lid and found it, lying crumpled on top.

She took it back to her chair and sat down, taking another sip from her coffee. The front said, "To Scout." Was this a prank? The inside was even more unbelievable:

We didn't exchange names, but you said you were right below me. I hope this is the young lady I woke on the beach yesterday afternoon. If it is, you will understand why I called you Scout. Wondered if we might share lunch by the pool. Maybe talk some more about books we've read?

Ben (a.k.a. spoiler of naps)

Alyce was dumbfounded and a little bit of something else she couldn't place. What was it her Irish friends said? *Gobsmacked!* She found herself looking around as if someone might be watching. That was silly, of course, but this was new territory.

She replayed their interaction, trying to recall anything she'd done to lead him on or suggest she was interested in him. It felt as if she'd been unfaithful to Michael simply by reading a piece of paper. She'd done nothing to solicit it. But why did she suddenly feel coquettish? Was she actually blushing, sitting all alone in a room where no one knew a thing?

Alyce needed to settle herself a bit. She jumped up from the chair and opened the patio doors to step out and calm her racing heartbeat. This was crazy. She inhaled deeply, raising her arms above her head in a morning stretch. As she brought her arms down slowly, reaching outward as they lowered to her side, she scanned the horizon where the water met the sky. A lone jet skier skimmed across the water, the buzzing sound of the motor carrying across the waves. She inhaled once more, her hands moving upward in a sweeping gesture, and relaxed through the exhale. There. That was better.

She stepped closer to the railing and became aware that someone was looking up at her. From her perch on the second-floor balcony, it took a minute to realize it was him. Ben. He appeared to be grinning at her. She shielded her eyes and waved. *Why did you do that?*

He carried a book in his right hand and a towel in his left. He lifted his book in greeting, and for half a moment, they stood there— until Alyce remembered she was still in her pajamas and hadn't combed her hair.

Abruptly, she stepped back, then thought maybe it seemed rude. She leaned forward, gave another wave, and ducked inside. What in the world was going on? Alyce was acting like a schoolgirl! And not a high schooler but a middle schooler! Where was the settled, middle-aged distraught woman who had arrived just two days before? And what were these feelings that seemed to be playing Jekyll and Hyde inside of her? She wasn't sure what was happening, but it all seemed directly related to this Ben person. She needed to nip this in the bud right away. She would dress, go down, and tell him she was a married woman.

But that wasn't true for long. Once she signed those papers, it would be over in a few short weeks. And all the poor guy wanted to do was have lunch. They weren't about to make out or get married or something.

The sudden *ding-ding* of an incoming text startled Alyce back to the moment. The phone on her bedside table became urgent with *ding-ding, ding-ding, ding-ding* as text after text landed. Good grief. Something must be going on. Instinctively, she knew Michael was summoning her. If it were the kids with that much to say, they would have called. The only way he had communicated with her for several months now, even before the big "reveal," was via text message. And the quick succession of dings usually meant he was heated about something.

Alyce was right, of course. She scanned the texts briefly. Apparently, Michael had found out he was going to be a grandpa but not from Maggie. And somehow this was inadvertently Alyce's fault. As she read the angry blurbs, she asked Jesus to please filter them and show her what, if any of it, needed a response.

Normally, she would have reread the texts several times, looking for clues as to how Michael was doing, what he was thinking, and whether he was missing her. But in that moment, she decided. She didn't have to address those texts as soon as they were received. In fact, she didn't have to address them at all. It was Michael's crisis.

Alyce quickly checked for any other messages or emails that needed her attention. She dropped her phone, a couple of magazines, and a fresh beach towel into her bag. She made sure she had plenty of sunscreen and lip balm, her extra room key, and a debit card in the little zippered purse she always carried in her bag to the beach.

Then Alyce went to her suitcase and picked out a swimsuit and matching cover-up. She brushed her teeth, shaved her legs, and applied some tinted moisturizer and waterproof mascara. A ponytail and baseball cap seemed like a good choice for the day. How about some sassy silver hoops to finish the picture?

She studied her reflection in the mirror and briefly felt sadness. She genuinely wished she could be enough for her husband. The girl looking back at her had only yesterday appeared tired and weary. Now, she felt hopeful at the visage before her. What had made the difference? Someone—some *man*—perhaps found her attractive. He at least found her worth sharing lunch.

Of course he doesn't really know you, she chided herself, then immediately checked that emotion. *I'm so sorry, Lord,* she prayed. *I have lost sight of the amazing creation You see when You look at me. Why is it so hard to acknowledge my worth? I thank You. I really, really thank You that I am more than I know.*

When she looked again, she saw a vibrant, intelligent gal who appeared excited and fresh-faced. What did she have to lose by sharing lunch? Apparently, at this point, not one thing. What did she have to gain? It seemed a new friend and a rejuvenated outlook on life—a terrific gain for little investment, just offering what she'd always been to a new audience.

Alyce made her way to the fridge and grabbed a cold bottle of water. Headed out, she almost forgot her sunglasses, but when she opened the door to the breezeway, the bright sun reminded her, and she turned back to retrieve them. *Ding-ding, ding-ding, ding-ding* came from her beach bag. Not more from Michael! As a last-minute impulse, she dug down to find her cell phone. Without one glance at the screen, she plopped it onto the counter and marched out the door.

Chapter Four

BEN

*B*en shielded his eyes and squinted up at the balcony where, just moments before, his newfound friend had stood. In the bright morning sun, she reminded him somewhat of the little dog in *How the Grinch Stole Christmas*, with her short, sheepish wave, just before she had scooted back inside the condo. He was amused by her. Intrigued, even.

They'd only met yesterday in a brief encounter. His buddy had slung the Frisbee wide right, and he dove to catch it. When he got up off the sand, he realized it had sailed past him and smacked into her beach chair.

As he ran to retrieve the disc, he'd prayed the woman asleep under the umbrella wasn't going to fly up and berate him with obscenities. He had a low tolerance for such women. After all, the Frisbee hitting her chair was an honest mistake. Ben had already begun formulating his rebuttal as he braced for a tongue-lashing.

He silently hoped perhaps she hadn't awakened at all, but it was not to be. She propped herself up and groggily looked around, apparently startled from a deep sleep. Her hair was a mess, and she moved like a character from *Night of the Living Dead*.

"Sorry about that," he'd muttered, steeling himself for her tirade. He attempted to reach for the Frisbee while avoiding eye contact. However, when she offered no reply, he glanced her way. She was still struggling to come fully awake.

Relieved that she was unaware of his presence, he stole another look. She was about his age, he guessed, with a wholesome prettiness accentuated by slight, sun-kissed freckles on her nose. She moved clumsily, but something about that made her disarming. However, she'd still not responded to being roused. Ben had learned the hard way that looks could be deceiving.

It turned out she was not an angry person. Their encounter had been brief, but their conversation led him to wonder about the possibility of another. Walking back to his game of Frisbee, he pondered the idea of asking her to lunch. He considered the fact that she might be married, but how would he know unless he asked? Nothing ventured, nothing gained.

As he slipped a note under her door that morning, he convinced himself this was the least awkward way to approach things. Knock and run. *Very mature*, he mused. He simultaneously whispered two prayers: "Lord, please let this be her condo," and, "Lord, what in the world am I doing?"

Now, Ben made his way to a bright blue umbrella protecting two lounge chairs from the sun. He had spent a restorative weekend with his friends. He considered himself overwhelmingly blessed to know three such caring men. Friendships like theirs were not at all common; this Ben knew very well.

Theirs was a brotherhood, bound by heartache and restoration. Each man brought his own mix of pain and deliverance to the group. The best part of their friendship was they had met after each had arrived at his own identity in Christ, each one unique as the prints their feet left in the sand.

Through them, Ben had found immense value in the human story. Where before he would categorize the ragtag group in a broad sweep of gender and privilege, he now saw the vivid details of multifaceted lives. He felt honored to join his story with theirs and humbled that they felt safe to do the same.

The four "brothers" had spent the long weekend deep-sea fishing, hanging out on the beach, and eating great seafood. Early that morning, before he'd packed them off to their responsibilities at home, they had gathered on the beach as the sun rose and prayed.

They thanked God and prayed for many things: for His Son who took their blame and their shame, leaving them unbound by their pasts to walk in freedom; for their families, that God would give them opportunities to restore relationships where they had inflicted so much pain; for each other and the permission they'd granted for accountability; and for safety in transparency as they sought to bring everything into the light.

Now, the remainder of his stay stretched before him. A time to consider what his next steps in life would be.

He thought about the wasted years that passed while he slowly came to the end of himself. Life had been very kind to him. Too kind, perhaps. He had devalued everything because of the ease with which he attained each level, conquered each relationship, and mastered each task. Ben worked hard and had much to show for it, but now he was lonely because of his past. Were it not for his relationship with Christ and the understanding that his past had been forgiven, he would have spiraled into a suicidal depression long ago.

Settling into the chair, Ben sank his feet into the warm sand and gazed into the horizon and the expanse of blue water before him. A familiar practice now, intentionally being still was a time to accept the new day and appreciate the gift of life, a chance to center and focus his thoughts on the true source of peace and joy and affirm his sufficiency in Christ.

Ben had known redemption in many areas in his life. Unfortunately, his marriage hadn't been one of them. It was his own doing—or undoing, you might say. An old, familiar angst crept into Ben's heart and threatened its usual tug of war with his psyche. He pulled out a phrase from scripture and silently repeated, *Lord, take every thought captive, take every thought captive...*

He closed his eyes and recalled a familiar hymn from his childhood. He had learned it at the country church that was such an integral part of his grandpa's life. Back then, Ben found amusement in the rhythmic way the older folks would sing it. He could now see how that familiar cadence helped bring the words to mind:

Redeemed! Redeemed! Redeemed by the blood of the Lamb!
Redeemed! Redeemed! His child and forever I am!

With eyes closed and head leaned back, Ben was still reminiscing when he sensed the presence of someone standing over him. Opening his eyes, Ben saw the silhouette of a large man shrouded in a halo of brilliant sunshine. He struggled to make out the face.

"I'm not here to pick a fight," a deep voice said. Instinctively, Ben moved to stand, but the much larger man told him to sit down. Ben's hairs stood up on his arms and legs, and his heart skipped a beat as he lowered himself obediently back into the chair. "I just need to speak my peace to you. Aren't you Ben Roberson?"

Not waiting for affirmation, the large man folded himself into the adjacent chair. Ben now turned to face him, eased by the fact that he'd chosen to come down to his level. The man was easily twice the size of Ben. He was slightly graying, and his eyes seemed kind. But Ben did not recognize him at all.

"Do I know you?" he asked tentatively. Life choices had caused Ben to be on his guard in situations such as this. He had thoughtlessly had multiple affairs over the years. More accurately, they were one-night stands. An affair required an investment of himself, something that never interested him. He'd been confronted by a spouse on more than one occasion. The crooked scar on his nose was permanent evidence from an encounter with one such husband.

"The name's James McDermott," came the reply. "My wife was Renee. Perhaps you remember her? Renee McDermott? I certainly hope so."

Ben's entire being tensed at the mention of Renee McDermott. The two of them had spent one night together during a long business trip a few years back, but she had left a lasting impression on him. He had presented at a conference in Seattle and handpicked Renee to accompany him and represent her department. It required that she speak, and she had done a beautiful job. Each night of the conference, she resisted Ben's advances, but on their final night there, relieved at having her presentation behind her, she indulged in a couple of glasses of champagne and succumbed to Ben's relentless pursuit.

After they returned to work, Renee had called him, frantic to see him again. Because she worked on an entirely different floor of Ben's company, their paths seldom crossed, which was a scenario that often played out to Ben's advantage.

Business trysts were meaningless to him, mere opportunities to feed his sexual appetite, regardless of the lives affected. He had become adept at squelching any attempts by hapless women who desired more. He could be a cruel boss. Why would the CEO engage in a long-term relationship with any of them? He had assumed Renee's repeated contacts were her desperate efforts to make a case for something more.

How many women had begged and pleaded for the same? How many felt they were "soul mates" and meant to be together forever? If he could delay meeting with them long enough, most of the women would get the message, become discouraged, or even move to another company. Who knew the talent he'd lost to competitors all because he couldn't master his sexual voracity? His addiction to pornography was only appeased through encounter after encounter, all the while avoiding intimacy.

Renee, however, was determined to see him. In his desperation to shut her up, Ben agreed. To his surprise, she didn't want to meet at a hotel but rather at a restaurant where many of their colleagues could potentially see them together. Why not? He agreed to meet for lunch. This was not normal, but in a twisted way, Ben found it dangerous and exciting.

Despite his risky behaviors, he assumed his reputation remained intact. Ben had a reputation alright, but not the one he imagined. He had no idea of the office chatter that circulated about him or the level of disrespect associated with his name. Had his company not been well established and reputable before he came on board, many of his colleagues would have abandoned ship along the way.

As he approached Renee at the table that day, he was surprised to find another woman also seated there. He quickly flipped through his mental file. She was about his age. Decently attractive. *Is this about to get interesting?* he thought in his perverted, selfish brain. He scanned the restaurant, praying he wouldn't see a familiar face. Not one person flashed across his radar. He relaxed.

Whether this lunch talk led to an afternoon of sex or another pitiful campaign speech for "Ben and Renee forever," this was nothing to him. He was a pro at lowering the boom on hapless women.

He sat down, placed his napkin in his lap, and casually opened his menu. As he perused the offerings there, Renee introduced the other woman as Jeanine and shared something about her being an accountability partner. He was not sure what that meant. Maybe Renee was an alcoholic? No matter.

Deciding on his order, he folded the menu and tossed it onto the table. Ben found it best to sit and listen in these settings, so he settled back and feigned interest.

Now that he knew Jeanine was not there for fun and games, he was prepared for Renee's pleas to see him again. He would save his rehearsed response for just the right moment when it would be unmistakable what his intentions had been: no "them," only him. She would likely burst into tears or explode in anger. Either way, she would quickly depart, leaving him to enjoy a nice prime rib sandwich. Maybe he'd even take time for one of those banana puddings they served in a mason jar before returning to the office. Ben couldn't care less about Renee.

He wondered if she had any idea he was married. He had long ago learned the rhythm of removing his wedding ring on the way to work and putting it back on the minute he was on the interstate headed home. This had been his routine for so long now he did it without thinking. He even had an answer for his wife, Amie, should she show up at the office, which she rarely did, and notice he wasn't wearing it.

"I've been in the warehouse," he'd say, reaching into his pocket and putting it back on. Warehouse rules were "no jewelry," to avoid any accidents around equipment. Ben seldom went near the machinery, but did occasionally pop in to check productivity. He justified it as theoretically possible and, therefore, not entirely a lie. He was a master at justifying his actions and had convinced himself that most men led double lives without consequence. So, why shouldn't he?

Ben flicked at an imaginary piece of lint on his pants, then tuned in to what was being said at the table. To his utter shock, Renee's words were not about him at all. Renee was apologizing for her behavior on their trip together. It was not who she was, nor did it represent who she belonged to. *Who she belonged to?* The conversation was getting weird very quickly. He shifted awkwardly in his seat, avoiding eye contact with either woman.

Renee rambled about them both being Christians and how sorry she was for leading him on. She had seen him out with his family one Sunday after church—she definitely knew about his wife and kids— and remembered how they held hands and prayed over their meal. She was struggling to handle her emotions and paused to gain composure. Jeanine reached over and squeezed her hand.

She continued, sharing how once, when she'd stopped by his office to try and talk, she'd seen pictures from a mission trip he'd taken to Honduras. What a horrible person she was to lead such a fine man of God astray!

Ben struggled to keep his jaw from dropping as he realized she was asking his forgiveness. She repeated her deep sorrow for acting selfishly and out of a dissatisfaction in her marriage.

"How can I make it right?" she asked.

Somewhere in the fog of shock, he realized she was offering to explain what had happened between them to Amie! It took an Academy Award-worthy performance to recover. Ben feigned his own grief over all that had transpired between them and assured her that he and Amie were handling things on their own.

That day in the restaurant with Renee was unsettling. It should have been a wake-up call, but he was so well ensconced in his own world of self that Ben could not be easily extracted. It would take something dramatic and life shattering to pull him out of the pit he'd fallen into. He plowed through many more lives before he finally grew sick of his own.

Ben shook himself to derail the train of memories and bring himself back to the reality of James there in the chair beside him. He hesitated to speak but knew he had to face the music. He still didn't understand what James McDermott was doing there on the beach. He'd been still and quiet, allowing Ben time to process whatever thoughts the mention of his wife's name had elicited.

"You said *was*," Ben half stated, half asked.

"Excuse me?" came the reply.

"Was. You said, 'Renee *was* my wife.' I most definitely remember Renee and her very pure heart. Unfortunately, I didn't know her in that regard. For that I am immeasurably sorry. I was under the impression that the two of you had remained married after our brief…affiliation. I have prayed many times that it would be so."

Ben slumped in his chair. Though he had rested well the previous night, he was suddenly weary from the realization that here sat another victim of his self-worship, of his callous lack of concern for consequences and the ripple effect they created. He lowered his head, squeezed his eyes tightly, and opened them again; whether to fight back the tears or in hopes that this was a bad dream, he did not know.

James' deep voice broke into Ben's consciousness. As he talked, Ben steeled himself for the diatribe but found, instead, that the words of this man fell softly as a peace offering between them. He loved his wife dearly and was devastated when he found out she'd been unfaithful to their vows. They had sought counseling and determined that both had guilt when it came to nurturing and protecting their relationship. Their marriage had ended stronger than they'd ever imagined.

"I don't understand," Ben said, with a look of total confusion mixed with sadness. "Why did your marriage end?"

James drew in a breath and then spoke with as much tenderness a man of his size could ever convey, "My Renee was diagnosed with stage 4 lung cancer last spring. She went home to the Lord just six months ago now."

Ben had always appreciated how the roar of the ocean provided a buffer for confidential conversations, but today he was grateful that it muffled the crying of two grown men. He collapsed his face into his hands as he heard the gentle sobs from a man whose massive size meagerly attempted to provide a home for his huge heart. James awkwardly patted Ben's shoulder with his giant paw of a hand. Ben's body heaved even harder at the thought of this man he had violated offering him consolation.

When it seemed all tears were spent, both men sat staring out at the ocean, content in the silence. At last, Ben spoke, "James, I…" he faltered for words.

"I know," James said.

"If I could…" he trailed.

"I would let you." James shook his head as he spoke, "Heck, I'd *make* you!"

Both men softly laughed as the freshness of a wrong made right washed over them. As James stood to go, Ben stood and offered his hand. James shook it and pulled him into a giant bear hug. He released him and said, "Thanks for hearing me out." He turned and headed back up the beach from wherever he had come.

Ben fell back into his chair. He felt as if he'd wrestled directly with God. He had a million thoughts clamoring for attention, not the least of which was, *Where had James even come from, and how did he recognize Ben there at the beach?*

Every thought fell captive to one central thought: *Why, in this mess of a life Ben had finally surrendered to God, did He delight him with moments such as these?* Renee had been a catalyst in Ben's life, but change would ultimately require far more because of the hardness of his heart.

Sadly, Ben's story would not include restoration with Amie, although he had desperately hoped. He bowed his head and breathed a prayer for James. He prayed for Amie and her husband, who was now raising his children. He prayed redemption of his relationship with his daughter and son. He had no doubt that God would continue to be faithful in all things.

Chapter Five

ALYCE

*A*lyce rode the elevator to the parking garage where she stopped to snag her favorite sunglasses from her car on the way to the beach. Glancing at the parking space assigned to Unit 302, she saw a Range Rover with a University of Alabama license plate. Of course that had to be his vehicle. Didn't he say he had attended Alabama? She added that to her list: cute, educated, *and* Southern.

She had decided she would accept his offer to share lunch. Why, she couldn't say. Perhaps in response to Michael's accusatory texts from this morning? Lunch with a perfect stranger was as naughty as Alyce would ever be, though unexpected enough to shock anyone who knew her well. Alyce decided in her matter-of-fact way that this would be her act of retaliation. She would have lunch with a man not her husband in a semi-exotic setting. She laughed at her attempt at moxie, as if a lunch date would ignite a scandal.

Alyce began making a list of questions to ask when they finally met. She'd become quite adept at deflecting the topic from herself. Being from the South would be a definite conversation starter. In fact, it could give them enough fodder to last through lunch. Just in case, she needed some backup topics. How would she keep the conversation moving?

Alyce reached into the pocket of her cover-up and pulled out the note to read the signature again: "Ben (a.k.a. spoiler of naps)." She needed to be certain she remembered his name at the very least.

I can't do this, Alyce thought. *It's all too overwhelming.*

By the time she made her way to the chairs she had rented for the week, she was in a tizzy. Her confidence, buoyed by her newly tapped anger at her husband, now seemed to have lost its steam. Everything about the past twenty-four hours was foreign and confusing. She'd pretty much been confused by life in general the past year. Why add more fuel to the fire by letting Michael push her to date again?

Alyce, that's ridiculous. She chided herself for being so dramatic. *You don't have to* do *anything. You don't have to* feel *anything. You can just be. That's why you're here, right?*

She looked at the row of beach chairs. Why did everything come in pairs and taunt her? She inhaled deeply and scolded herself for being so dramatic. What was up with her emotional extremes? She'd experienced panic, anger, sassiness, and doubt, all within a matter of minutes.

Alyce casually scoured the beach for her new friend, Ben. In the early-April lull between spring-break rush and summertime madness, the area wasn't super crowded. She admired the smart line of blue umbrellas and matching chairs, which looked somewhat like an image on a mass-produced postcard. But if he was under one of those, Alyce couldn't see him.

She dropped her bag beside her chair and removed her cover-up. Thinking twice about it, she put it back on, convincing herself the morning breeze was still a little cool, rather than owning the fact that she felt insecure in her swimsuit.

Alyce casually sat on the side of her chair, facing up the beach. From behind her baseball cap and sunglasses, she hoped to catch a view of those seated under the duos of umbrellas to her left. Only two sets were occupied. One by a couple she'd not seen before. Beside the other, Chloe and her dad were creating a sandcastle.

Seeing the two of them made Alyce daydream about bringing her own grandchild to the beach for the first time. Maybe Chloe's pink flamingo swimsuit made Alyce imagine a little girl. Maggie was all about pink and tutus and bows—the bigger the better. A girl would surely be an easy fit for her daughter. Any girls born to Lillian would be another story entirely as Lillian loathed pink and preferred climbing trees to tea parties. But it would be a while before she had to worry over a child for her younger daughter, who was busy working on graduating college—specifically preparing for her senior show.

Alyce grabbed her phone, checked the time, and dialed Lillian's number. Although she'd earlier slammed it on the counter and stormed out the door, she made it as far as the elevator when she remembered she needed it for their morning chat. She had to retrieve it because she never missed calling her girls.

One of her new promises to herself was that she would cease to react to Michael. She would weigh out her decisions and *act* but not *react*. No good ever came from her reactions. A feeling of empowerment washed over her when she had put the phone on "do not disturb" and stuffed it back into her bag, rather than reacting to his texts. She was learning.

Alyce knew her daughters well, including their schedules. Lillian would have just finished her eight o'clock class and be sitting in the student center drinking coffee and eating a bagel. That girl loved her bagels.

"Hi, Mom!" came the garbled but cheery voice as Lillian answered the phone. "Sorry, I just took a bite of bagel."

Alyce smiled. Oh, how she loved her children. They were fun and smart and talented. She knew she was prejudiced, but they were all three pretty, too. Harrison would have been highly upset that she called him pretty, but that's just what they were to her. The prettiest children ever.

"Hello, baby. How's my favorite middle child?"

"Mom?" Lillian said. "You sound very…content."

"I am content. Why wouldn't I be?"

"Umm, remember how pathetic you were when you left two days ago? Here I have been worried about you, and you sound better than I've heard in a long time."

"Who isn't content at the beach? And was I really pathetic?" Alyce asked, trying to control the sound of her voice. It threatened to expose the fact that a lunch invitation had positively redirected her thoughts from the chaos of her personal life. She had gone from anger to intrigue to trepidation to frustration and back to intrigue, and all before lunchtime!

"Well, something sounds different. I'm not sure what it is, but there's definitely a new tone to your voice. What have you been up to?"

"Nothing!" was Alyce's retort. She realized that Lillian was merely asking what was up. No implications. She hoped the abruptness of her reply would go unnoticed. Just in case, Alyce quickly forged ahead, "Not a blooming thing. Isn't it wonderful?"

Lillian's voice sounded slightly doubtful, but she graciously refrained from any further comments. "That is wonderful, Mom. I'm happy to hear you relaxed. How's the weather?"

"Couldn't be better. The only thing that would make me happier would be having you sitting here in the chair next to mine."

Lillian let out a blowing sigh, "Don't I wish?"

"You are close to the finish line, Lilli. This will be so worth all the effort. I cannot wait to see your beautiful artistry. Have you decided what you'll wear for your show?"

"They recommend we wear black because it won't detracts from my art."

"Then I shall wear black as well," Alyce announced. "Something celebratory and black, mind you, but black does make sense. Anything else going on?"

Alyce stood and walked to the ocean. The cool water glided toward her toes, and she did a little skip back from the sudden shock. Turning, she meandered along the water's edge as they continued talking.

"I had dinner with Dad last night."

Lillian's statement hung between them briefly. Every mention of Michael was a litmus test. How will Mom react if I say *Dad*? Is it okay if I do? Alyce noted that for the first time in a long while she felt nothing.

"Oh, yeah? What did y'all eat?"

"Well, I was busy working in the studio, and he just showed up with a pizza. It was kind of weird but good. I think pizza was his peace offering."

"Why would pizza be a peace offering?"

Lillian replied with a tone of confession in her voice, "I sort of read him the riot act because he didn't return Maggie's calls. She was trying to tell him about the baby and when she—"

"Over the phone?" Alyce interrupted indignantly.

"No, ma'am." Now Lillian defended. "She was going to have lunch with him and tell him. He wouldn't take her calls. Maggie knew he was ignoring her because his phone would ring once, then go straight to voicemail."

"She should have left him one."

"She did! He never really explained to me what happened, just said he was incredibly sorry and that it wouldn't happen again."

Alyce found it foreign, but she honestly didn't care why he wouldn't respond. She was mildly annoyed that he didn't take Maggie's call, but she knew he was awful about checking his phone to see if he'd missed anything. Typically, you either got him or you didn't, but if you didn't and you wanted a response, you had to call back.

A small flock of white birds scampered across the receding waves. Alyce reflexively opened her mouth to remind her daughter of her daddy's idiosyncrasies, then thought better of it. *Michael is not my responsibility,* she reminded herself. She would have to retrain her married muscles.

At that precise moment, Alyce looked up to see Ben in conversation with a very large man. They were sitting under the next to last umbrella down the beach from her chair. She froze on the spot. What should she do? Keep strolling and try to act natural? Turn around and head back to her chair? She was uncertain if he had seen her. Whatever they were discussing appeared pretty serious.

"Hello? Mom?"

Alyce snapped to and realized Lillian had been talking the entire time.

"Baby, I am so sorry. I was distracted by something going on down the beach and totally missed what you said."

Alyce hoped Lillian wouldn't ask *what* was going on. Fortunately for her, Lillian suddenly interjected, "It's okay, Mom. I just realized the time. Sorry! I've got to run. Love you!"

"Love you, too!" Alyce said. And just like that, her middle child was off to conquer the world.

She lowered her phone to put it away, then thought better of it. She returned it to her ear and tried to walk nonchalantly along the water's edge. Alyce stopped and turned to the condos, feigning an intense interest in describing the resort property to her imaginary friend on the other end of the line.

This vantage point provided enough of a view that, from the corner of her eye, she could see the two men hunkered down under the next to last umbrella. Once again, her hat and glasses came in handy and provided a nice foil for her spying, although the pair appeared oblivious to everyone else on the beach.

She couldn't stare, for Pete's sake, but was Ben crying? How odd. Her curiosity was beginning to get the better of her. Whatever could the two men be discussing?

Alyce's thoughts were abruptly interrupted by a sudden burst of laughter. Chloe's mother had arrived, and the pair were racing in and out of the ocean, playing a game of cat and mouse with the waves.

Their actions triggered a sweet memory of Michael and their girls doing the same as Alyce sat on the beach holding baby Harrison. She was transported to another time and place in an idyllic past, full of joy and love.

Michael would take turns lifting each girl and swinging them in a circle over his head. Cries of, "My turn, Daddy!" slid over the foamy sound of surf as each one raised her hands to be whisked away by their father. Michael turned to wave at her and their new son, his tan, handsome face beaming as he raced toward both girls, scooped them up collectively, and ran into the ocean to their delighted squeals.

Her heart caught in her throat, and she brushed away tears that leaked from her eyes before she realized. Alyce made a beeline for the safety of her chair, hoping to hide before the dam burst and she became a blubbering mess.

She realized that she was still holding the phone to her ear. It reminded her of the many times she'd imagined the man she'd loved for thirty years calling her to return. She could hear his voice, even after these nine months of brutal separation, declaring what a fool he was. In her dream world, he would assure her their marriage was worth the fight.

Alyce had to face facts. She was alone at fifty. For the first time in over half her life, she had no one clamoring for her attention—no kids, no husband. Yesterday she had deemed this a good thing. Now it only made her heartbeat reverberate within her hollow insides like the sound of footsteps in an empty house.

Alone.

Unlovable.

Old.

Used up.

She put her phone away and gathered her things to head inside. Although she'd been on the beach for less than an hour, this was not the place for a full-blown emotional breakdown, and Alyce knew the warning signs.

Her eyes fell upon a small leather book inside her bag. It contained scripture she often read aloud for strength. Everywhere she went, Alyce tried to keep the book with her. A gift from her best friend to help navigate adjustment to an empty nest, she'd received it when Harrison was about to start his senior year in high school.

The verses were arranged by topic, and Alyce found many of them helpful throughout her day. The soft cover was supple from frequent use. Neither she nor her friend had any idea how empty the nest was going to be.

In August of the previous year, she and Michael had driven their son to Knoxville to the University of Tennessee and helped arrange his room for the start of his freshman year. They'd treated him to dinner then left as he waved goodbye on the curb. Alyce had cried most of the way home. Yes, she was sad to leave her last baby at college. But also, the three-hour drive back to Nashville was when she initially confronted Michael about her findings.

Lately, Alyce had been memorizing the verses on fear. She had discovered that fear was the root of many volatile emotions. Her go-to verse was 1 John 4:18, "There is no fear in love. Perfect love casts out fear."

She grabbed the tiny volume and flipped it open, removing her sunglasses and wiping her eyes. The words of truth she read welled up inside her and filled the microscopic cracks in her soul where the enemy planted weeds of doubt and bitterness.

Her friend had written these words inside the cover: "When the liar is overwhelming and begins harvesting a crop of lies, feast on this and remember what he says is never what God says. Be still and tune your heart to God and expect the truth. He gets the final say, Alyce. He loves you, and He will strengthen you with words that speak life to your soul. Ask Him to show you."

Alyce settled back into the chair and resisted the urge to flee. The enemy had far too many notches in his belt for battles he'd initiated and won in her life. The desire to run away was replaced with something gentle but strong. It beckoned her to stay and enjoy the beauty before her. For months she had prayed to be still while God fought for her. Was this the peace of finally surrendering her weapons to Him?

She softly read aloud the verses that satisfied her inner longings. She inserted her name and changed the pronouns, a practice she'd adopted that personalized the scriptures in a tangible way:

"I won't let you down; Alyce, I won't leave you."

"Alyce, I love you with an everlasting and eternal love."

"I have not given you a spirit of fear, Alyce, but a spirit of power, love, and a sound mind."

She read until she found herself asking, "Father, what do *You* say about me?" Each gentle reply in her spirit spun her around with His love.

Beloved.

Treasured.

Beautiful.

Mine.

Now her tears flowed freely. Only this time the tears were not from anger or defeat. The tears were because she had remembered His promises.

A few months prior, Alyce had read these words in Malachi: "Test me in this and see if I will not open the windows of heaven and pour out a blessing." She knew the passage referenced God's promise concerning tithing. But she also knew many other places in scripture where God extended an invitation to test His promises and see.

As she read the verses on fear aloud, she found herself replaying the times He had proven true to His Word in her life. She imagined God speaking, "Remember, Alyce, that time you needed and I gave, but what I gave was much better? Don't forget to remember My promises. I am the faithful one."

She found peace in testing the Lord's promises and joy in the evidence of His faithfulness. As the brilliant sunshine bathed her body in warmth, so the beauty of the Holy Spirit warmed her innermost being, dispelling the doubts and troubles that threatened her.

Alyce lost track of the time as she closed her eyes and rested. In spring, the ocean breeze could sometimes be cool. She was grateful the sun's warmth wrapped around her like a blanket. It made her cozy and sleepy. She felt she could linger forever.

Alyce frowned as a cloud blocked the sun. Turning her face upward, she opened one eye in frustration, but no cloud was blocking the sun. Instead, Alyce found herself peering at Ben.

She immediately sat up and rubbed her hands over her face as if she could remove traces of her emotions. She quickly replaced her sunglasses in an attempt to hide. It was much like the day before when they had met. She was groggy then, too, but she hadn't been crying. Today, they had both been crying.

Unfazed, he plopped into the chair beside her. He looked straight out at the ocean and said, "Well, isn't this a lovely day at the beach?"

Alyce had no words, so she turned toward the ocean as well and nodded her head in agreement.

Whatever she thought this trip was going to be, she hadn't factored him into the equation. But then again, she *had* told the Lord she was open to whatever He wanted to do. And if she knew one thing about God, she knew He was always full of surprises.

Turning toward her new friend, she stuck out her hand and said, "I'm Alyce Keriman."

"Ben," he said as he faced her, "Ben Roberson." But instead of simply shaking her hand, he grasped it in a hand hug and patted it in comfort. Alyce received his comfort. God was full of surprises indeed.

Chapter Six

MICHAEL

*M*ichael backed through the glass door to the conference room. On one hand he balanced two boxes of pastries and in the other a mug of steaming hot coffee prepared by his assistant, Carrie.

She deserved a raise. For one so young, she represented Michael well in the professional manner he prized. And after only a brief time, she'd quickly learned the mechanics of being his administrative assistant. Since her predecessor retired, he'd interviewed many candidates and hired and fired two before landing on her. The others had proven proficient in some areas but weren't the whole package. He had been afraid some unexposed quality would necessitate firing her. But to date, she was ideal, and he was beginning to relax and enjoy all she brought to the table.

Carrie was a newlywed, and her husband was in law school. She was willing to work long hours since he was in the library most evenings. Michael tried not to abuse her availability. He wanted her at home whenever her husband was free. He remembered those days and the demands of law school on his time. In many ways, she reminded him of his own girls, and he would have hoped the same consideration for them.

"Good morning, Mr. Keriman!"

Two interns jumped to their feet as he made his way into the beautifully decorated chrome and glass room. Floor-to-ceiling windows provided unobscured views of the Cumberland River and the Titans stadium, where Michael owned a box and spent many Sundays entertaining clients.

Alyce had handled the office decor for him. A few years back, she insisted he update from the stuffy darkness of the nineties to a contemporary look with clean lines. It suited Michael perfectly and gave him just the edge he needed to feel accomplished. She liked to say he was empowered by a mighty God. These days Michael just felt powerful.

There were several junior partners around the massive conference table, chatting amongst themselves. Michael called these meetings at will to review cases and keep his associates on their toes. It also kept him abreast of some of his larger clients' files.

His inability to handle each case for himself was a sore spot. He had yielded only after the doctor warned he was running a high risk of a heart attack. Stress had been through the roof, and he could either choose to back off or his body would make the decision for him.

He couldn't explain the anxiety. He had a thriving practice, with money in the bank. He had a gorgeous young woman as his companion, and his children seemed content.

If Michael's doctor caught sight of his gooey delights from Sugarloaf Bakery, he would launch into him without mercy. He knew better than to even steal a taste of one of their famous cinnamon rolls, one of several delicacies he had chosen for the office. The warmth of the box on his hand was merciless in its taunting. He could imagine a hot donut dipped into his coffee. It would demand great restraint not to indulge.

Of course, he now had a grandchild on the way. He had every intention of being around a long time and staying healthy to enjoy playing with him or her. Even before their own children were born, Michael and Alyce had planned for grandchildren. They'd made a pact to take each grandchild on a special trip when he or she turned thirteen. He intended to keep that plan in place, even though divorced. He didn't have any idea how they'd make it happen, but somehow they would. That was a problem for another day.

As everyone took their seats, Michael looked around the table. He immediately noticed that Cassidy was missing.

"Where is Miss Simpson?"

One of the associates spoke up, "I heard her say something about an appointment this morning."

Michael was unaccustomed to anyone missing his meetings. All his people canceled appointments whenever they conflicted with work. He and Cassidy hadn't talked since he abruptly left her at the restaurant. After pizza with Lillian, he had headed straight back to his apartment. She wasn't there.

He had texted her. She responded she'd left shortly after he did to go out with girlfriends. Explaining she would be spending the night with one of them, she told him not to wait up. He couldn't tell if she might be pouting. Not one for texting, Michael had left it at that. Their relationship was not exclusive, though most nights she could be found at his place.

He was not pleased with her absence from work but felt a tinge of guilt at leaving her the way he had. For a moment, it struck him that he viewed one young employee as a daughter and another as his girlfriend.

The revelation irritated him, so he pushed it aside, opened a folder, and launched into his meeting.

They had been working for some time and had discussed almost every case when he noticed Carrie standing outside the glass wall of the conference room, willing him to look at her. Once she caught his glance, she gently tapped her wrist as if to remind him of the time. He nodded to her in acknowledgement but wasn't sure what she was implying.

Michael punched the button on his phone lying next to a stack of files. 12:07. He tried to recall if he was supposed to be somewhere. If so, it eluded him, but he knew if Carrie was signaling, he needed to wind things up.

He decided to launch into one more item. "Where are we on Mrs. Burdeshaw's will revisions?" Flipping to the front of the file, he saw that it had been assigned to Cassidy. Since she wasn't there, he was about to move on when one of the interns spoke.

"I met with her last week and will be sending over the revisions for her to review this afternoon."

Michael stared at the young man as if he'd said, "I convinced Mrs. Burdeshaw to cut off her head."

"What did you say?" he demanded, a scowl darkening his visage.

The intern pulled himself straight up in his chair and tried to sound more efficient. "I spoke with her last week and—"

"I heard what you said," Michael interrupted. "What I'm wondering is why you are addressing a case to which you have not been assigned."

The young man was confounded. Michael's intimidating look left him dazed. The buzz of quiet conversation immediately muted.

"Remind me of your name, son."

"Dylan Harper," he stated, sounding somewhat like a witness taking the stand.

"Mr. Harper," Michael growled, "why did you have a conversation with Mrs. Burdeshaw when this client was specifically assigned to Miss Simpson?"

Every pair of eyes was fixed on a file. No one dared to look in the direction of their boss, who was known for his arched eyebrow. You positively did not want to bear the brunt of it. You could feel the eyebrow, even if you didn't see it. To his credit, Dylan Harper didn't break eye contact.

"Cassidy asked me to take it since she is busy with the, uh, busy with the..." his voice trailed as he realized he was not helping things.

At that exact moment, Carrie opened the door and said, "Pardon me, Mr. Keriman, but your lunch appointment has arrived."

Michael did not remember an appointment, but, fortunately for Dylan Harper, he knew Carrie wouldn't interrupt if it wasn't important. She hurried away as he gathered his files, grabbed his phone, and walked out. A collective sigh could be heard, though premature.

Michael turned around, pushed open the door, and glared around the room. "This meeting is not adjourned. Go to lunch, but do not take more than one hour. We will resume precisely at one thirty." He fixated on the intern. "And, Mr. Harper? We will begin with the matter at hand."

With that, he headed down the hallway toward his office where he encountered Carrie rounding her desk to meet him. The sight of her made him relax his demeanor and change his tone. Perhaps she was even going to be good for his blood pressure.

"Carrie, for the life of me, I cannot recall making a lunch appointment."

He followed her gaze to look toward his office door. "Your daughter is here?" she spoke hesitantly. "You told me that family takes precedence over anything. I should always interrupt. I wondered if perhaps you had forgotten to put it on your calendar."

Because his hands were full, she swung open the door to his office. Inside, he found Maggie with a big bag from one of their favorite lunch spots. She stood and greeted them both with a warm smile and thanked Carrie for retrieving her dad.

"Do you need anything for your picnic?" Carrie seemed delighted they were having one. "I can grab you some sweet tea or lemonade." She relieved Michael of his files and waited.

Maggie was glowing. He could see it immediately. She was beautiful, and for a moment, he was struck by how much she resembled her mother. His voice caught in his throat as he said, "I'll have a water, and she'll have . . " He coughed. "These allergies are going to kill me." He walked to her and wrapped her in a big hug. "Ginger ale, am I right?" He looked down at his oldest daughter.

"You know me well, Daddy. Do you have some?"

"I always have ginger ale for my girl."

Carrie left them alone. Michael felt all stress release from his body as he sat down across from his daughter at the table and chairs in his massive office. A napkin and other utensils were neatly arranged in front of him. He was wearing a grin as Maggie opened his salad and tossed it the way she knew he liked it. She looked up and caught his gaze.

"What?"

"You'll always be my little girl, but you've become such a beautiful young woman. I was just remembering the first time I had that revelation. We were standing in the bridal suite, and I was about to give you away. Now you're going to be a mother. You are radiant."

Maggie blushed. His heart stirred again, and this time, he could not hide the tears as they sprang to his eyes. Gratitude and melancholy mingled as he realized she was now bound to his son-in-law in a unique and sacred way. They were going to be parents. Time could not be rewound. Moments could not be relived except as memories. He longed for the shallow waters of her childhood where he could keep her safe while she played freely.

"Jackson is very blessed that you chose him to be your husband."

"Well, that street goes two ways, Daddy," she said. "Jackson is a very fine man, and I love him with all my heart."

"I know you do, sweetheart. You guys have something special."

"Luckily, I found someone like you, Daddy."

Maggie's softly spoken compliment hung in the air as the full weight of what that could potentially mean in her life suddenly struck them both in different ways. The silence passed as they allowed the heaviness of truth to land. How awkward to think that Jackson could be just like him. The idea fell like a stone into the serenity between them. For a moment, they sat pensively as the ripples of thoughts unbidden threatened their happy mood.

Carrie entered with their drinks, and Michael adeptly switched gears in the conversation, deflecting attention back onto Maggie. They talked about when she'd found out she was pregnant, how she'd told Jackson, and how difficult it was to wait to tell everyone.

They laughed at Harrison's response when he received the news that he was going to be an uncle. Amidst the celebration, the full weight of it had suddenly registered, and he exclaimed with wide-eyed wonder, "That means you're going to be a mom!"

A sweet lunch, no mention was made of missed phone calls or unanswered texts between them. He'd always imagined such occasions since the time Maggie had gone away to college. He'd even dreamt this very scenario of sharing lunch in the office and having adult conversation with his daughter.

"Mom has already begun plans to turn my room into a nursery," Maggie shared. "She said she'd get to work on it as soon as she's back from the beach. I can't wait to see what she does. She's so creative."

"Oh? Your mom's at the beach? Lillian mentioned something about that last night."

Michael spoke as casually as he could. He tried to recall a time Alyce had ever gone on a trip by herself. He assumed she was not alone but with girlfriends. He could picture them all sitting around in their pajamas commiserating and raking him over the coals.

"She just took some time to think," Maggie said as she replaced the lid on her salad bowl and began clearing their trash. She intentionally didn't share more. She hoped he'd ask for details, which he did in a roundabout way.

"How much thinking can she get done with a posse of hens traveling with her?" he smirked.

"Oh, she went alone. I'm super proud of her. She arranged all the travel and was packed before any of us could say a thing. Not that we would, mind you. You know Mom. She's always been independent and determined when her mind is made up."

Stubborn and *bossy* were words Michael would have used, but never had he seen his wife as *independent*. He wasn't sure how he felt about her traveling alone. She would talk to anyone and could be far too trusting of strangers. He would go online and check their account. That would tell him where she was staying.

It briefly crossed his mind that he shouldn't be concerned with his soon-to-be ex-wife's antics. He justified it by reminding himself that, since she was unemployed, he was footing the bill for her little vacation.

"Will you be at Lilli's show?" Maggie interrupted his thoughts.

"Of course I will! I am eager to see her work gathered in one place," Michael replied.

He walked to his desk and pulled up the calendar on his computer. He clicked on May 24 and went to six thirty on Thursday. "Lillian's Senior Show," he typed. On the Monday before, he made a note to order flowers for her. He then asked Maggie, "What is your due date?"

"September 14," Maggie replied.

Michael went to September on his screen and laughed as he typed "Maggie due" on the fourteenth. "That's awfully close to Labor Day. Let's hope you don't choose then to go into labor. Are you guys telling names yet?"

"We honestly haven't decided."

"Well, your mother loved family names, which is why you guys are Margaret and Lillian and Harrison. But she graciously let me choose your middle names, subject to her approval, of course. She preferred short names for you girls, like Ann or Sue or Lynn, since you'd likely give those up when you married. The discussion could get intense. But by the time you arrived, your names were natural to call: Margaret Ann; Lillian Marie; Harrison Blake."

Michael stood to tell Maggie goodbye. It had done him good to share time with his daughter. As soon as she left, he picked up his phone and called Harrison, hoping to make plans to share a meal with him. It would be nice to drive to Knoxville for a day trip. While he waited to leave a message on Harrison's voicemail, he glanced at the clock in the top corner of his computer. It read 1:52.

Michael had his entire staff waiting on him to appear in the conference room. They would be relieved by his improved demeanor. He was surprised by his lack of urgency to return to the meeting.

He called Carrie into his office. "I'm leaving for the day. Once I'm gone, dismiss everyone waiting for me in the conference room. And tell Mr. Harper he and I will discuss his revisions to Mrs. Burdeshaw's will. Tomorrow."

He placed the file in the center of his desk, double-checked his afternoon schedule, then walked out of the office, oblivious to the souls barely breathing as he passed the conference room windows. Michael was done with work for the day.

Chapter Seven

BEN

*B*en drove his Range Rover into the assigned spot. He reached across the seat and grabbed a lush bundle of peonies in a translucent vase the color of sea glass. Flipping the visor one last time, Ben checked his hair and teeth before heading to the resort's outdoor restaurant. He glanced at his watch: 6:27. Pretty much right on time, just the way he liked it.

He approached the girl at the hostess stand, and she smiled. Everyone smiled whenever Ben came around. He had that eternal surfer boy look. His wavy hair matched the colors of the sand, which helped disguise the gray that had begun to mingle there. He wore a light blue, linen shirt, a crisp contrast to his deep tan. With the sleeves rolled twice, it conveyed the right mix of style and casualness. Ben was a congenial person, and his blue eyes always seemed to twinkle, conveying his overall happiness.

"Reservation for Ben Roberson," he said as he scanned the open restaurant, a practice he'd yet to shed from his philandering days. Back then, he had to make sure no one might recognize him. If he encountered a familiar face, he'd need to pull out one of his well-rehearsed explanations for why he was dining alone with a woman who wasn't his wife.

Slightly early for dinner, beach time, the restaurant was only half full. Ben had requested a specific table, where he knew the sunset would be best viewed, but saw that someone else was seated there.

"Right this way, Mr. Roberson. Your guest has already arrived."

As he followed the hostess, Ben looked around again. He hadn't noticed Alyce when he scanned the restaurant, yet he realized he might not spot her immediately in something other than her swimsuit, ponytail, and sunglasses—all he knew of her from their previous two encounters.

He had almost missed her altogether that morning. After James McDermott walked away, Ben had much to process, which was understandable after such an emotional exchange. There were more questions for which he needed answers. He walked down the beach in the direction he'd seen him go, but James was nowhere in sight.

Perhaps in his emotional state he'd been confused, and James had gone the other way. He reversed and took a few steps while scanning the folks gathered on the beach. That was when he spotted her, sitting under her umbrella.

Her head was tilted back against the cushion, her eyes closed. The last thing he wanted to do was wake her after the Frisbee incident the day before. From his vantage point, she appeared relaxed. That was a good sign. He really wanted to talk with her.

As Ben drew closer, he thought better of interrupting. Her face was slightly red and puffy as if she'd been crying. Perhaps some sudden loss had brought her here to the beach to mourn. She appeared to be traveling alone. Again, that urge to engage her nudged him. Ben wondered if they might be good company. What did he have to lose?

Before he could speak, Alyce opened her eyes. He had startled her. She quickly put on her sunglasses as he lowered himself into the seat on the other side of the umbrella. The two of them sat, fixed on the ocean, content in the silence. Neither seemed to have the capacity for words. After a long silence, Ben glanced sideways and realized she was looking at him.

"So," she said, "How's *your* day going?" That was when she'd stuck out her hand and told him her name.

"Ben Roberson," he'd replied.

At that, she'd cocked her head to the left and given him a wry smile. Ben felt the tension recede. They'd eased into a casual conversation about the resort and vacations and such, while carefully avoiding the serious topic of whatever had brought her to tears. Ben remained unaware she'd seen his encounter with James McDermott.

They were on the very safe subject of sunscreen when Alyce's stomach suddenly growled. Her eyes widened as she explained she'd skipped breakfast. Ben had been wondering how to broach the subject of the invitation to lunch he'd slipped under her door. "Shall we?" he simply asked as he stood. They moved to the poolside grill for lunch and talked for over an hour. She seemed to have quite an interest in all things Southern.

Alyce's phone chimed, and she jumped to her feet.

"I booked a massage!" she said proudly as she gathered her things and motioned for the check. With a flourish of her signature, she turned to go, but Ben stopped her.

"Do you have dinner plans?"

"No, but sounds great," she'd gushed. A light crimson crept up her cheeks. She was cute. Ben found it refreshing that he no longer evaluated women in his former crude ways. He genuinely wanted to know more about Alyce.

"Sushi at Red Fish at six thirty?" he'd asked.

"I've never had sushi a day in my life, but why not? I will see you there." And with that, she was gone. Ben looked down at her signature. Alyce H. Keriman. He put it into his phone with plans to search for her online. That was a place to begin.

~~~~~~~~~~

"Here we are," the hostess said as she stopped beside the very table he'd requested and pulled out the empty chair.

Ben turned to apologize to the young woman seated there and correct the hostess when he stopped short. A sly smile spread across his face as he shook his head. Now he understood.

"Is there a problem, sir?"

Alyce smiled back at him as he took the empty seat.

"Do you like it?" Alyce asked, waving her hand beside her new hairdo with a flourish. She remembered Ben had only seen her twice, and both times her hair had been in a ponytail. "I've worn my hair the same way for twenty-five years now," she explained. "I decided I needed a change. I did layers, highlights, the works!"

Ben mouthed, "Wow," as he nodded his head in affirmation.

"Is that a *wow* wow, or an *uh-oh* wow?" She knew.

Ben was not prepared for how genuinely beautiful Alyce was. The aquamarine dress she was wearing made her eyes sparkle. He became aware that he was staring and she was growing uncomfortable. And the hostess was still rather confused by it all.

He looked up at her and said, "This is exactly the table I hoped for. My apologies."

As she walked away, he turned to Alyce. "You look absolutely gorgeous, stunning, in fact."

Alyce couldn't remember ever being called stunning, or gorgeous for that matter. She glowed under his words.

"Are those for me?" she asked, tilting her head to one side.

Ben placed the vase of peonies on the table, "They are indeed."

"How'd you know peonies are my favorite?" she asked as she cupped one of the lovely blooms in her hand, then let her fingertips brush the delicate petals.

"Well, I must confess to a bit of Facebook stalking," Ben admitted. "You're a pretty open book there."

Alyce was quiet as her mind raced to recall her Facebook page. What all would he have gleaned from seeing her profile? Ben mistook her silence for disapproval and silently kicked himself for being so forward.

"I didn't exactly *stalk* you—just scrolled through enough to see that you love college football, particularly the Georgia Bulldogs, which is surprising since you grew up in Alabama. Did you graduate from Georgia?" He couldn't believe they hadn't covered that topic at lunch.

The transition to talk of football and college seemed to help Alyce relax, and the smile returned to her face. Their conversation flowed more organically. The two of them had as much in common as they were different.

He had traveled to many countries. Alyce hadn't traveled much outside of the South. She'd always wanted to, but life hadn't allowed much space for it. She was now, however, ready to explore more of the world.

Ben told Alyce of the fun she would experience in new places and cultures. The way Santorini rose out of the Mediterranean in dazzling white. How Budapest was actually two cities combined: Buda and Pest. Buda had been the ancient city of the royals, and the castle there sparkled when the sun hit it just right across the Danube. He spoke of Australian rain forests and the beauty of the Grand Canyon. The snowy white peacefulness of the Alps and the way the bison block the road, stopping all traffic in Yellowstone.

Alyce listened in rapt attention at Ben's animated descriptions. Finally, she shared that she had three children, two girls and a boy. They had been her whole life for over half of her life. With her oldest at twenty-five and her youngest at nineteen, she was trying to embrace this new season. Ben realized the level of commitment Alyce had given to her family. He applauded her sacrifice and love. He told her he had two children himself: a son and a daughter.

~~~~~~~~~~

Talk about children made Ben sad. He never realized how lonely Amie had been all those years he'd traveled. She wanted to adopt even before their kids were born, but Ben could never see his way clear to embrace the adoption process.

The two of them took extravagant vacations together. He told her they'd never be able to do this once they had children. She pressed him on many occasions. Once she became pregnant, she finally quit mentioning adoption.

Ben travelled more and more frequently for business. Those trips didn't align with her schedule as a pediatric intensive care nurse, so he went without her. He felt her work provided ample opportunities to surround herself with children, and soon she'd be busy with their own little girl. Their daughter was born and, shortly after, Ben had his first, brief affair. They went to counseling, and things got better for a while.

Business trips replaced their personal trips together. She filled her time with their daughter, and he traveled alone. That's when he'd been seduced by the allure of secret trysts. Lying to Amie became a fascinating game that gave him a sick thrill.

He now realized what a selfish pig he'd been, but so much in his life had been too little, too late. That was the old Ben, before he'd experienced grace. That Ben was badly deceived and duped into trading a future with a truly precious woman for the gratification that came through meaningless sexual encounters.

Thankfully, Amie had experienced emotional healing as she met and married a good man. Even so, she had been forever affected by his indiscretions, not only because he had broken her heart but also because Ben left her with a permanent physical reminder, a transmitted reminder that required medication for the rest of her life.

Ben was eternally grateful that he was not defined by his past. He had been a horrible monster by his own definition. Today, by grace, he walked free from everything that had kept him bound for so long. He knew he still had much to learn from his mistakes.

He felt certain God was going to use him to speak truth into the lives of young husbands. Though being so transparent after years of secrets was not something that came naturally to him, he was ready and willing to discuss his past if it saved one young man from following his broken path.

~~~~~~~~~

Ben realized he had grown quiet. Alyce seemed content to wait for him to rejoin their conversation. He was thankful to be sitting in a beautiful setting with a lovely new friend.

He and Alyce talked more about their lives. Their hobbies: hers was decorating; his was photography. Talents: he could play the saxophone while Alyce insisted she had none. And work: he shared modestly about his "little" company, which was, in truth, worth millions. Alyce told him about her work at Vanderbilt before coming home to be with their children, both jobs important to her.

They carefully avoided the discussion of spouses or significant others. Ben had seen pictures online of folks he presumed were Alyce's family. This included a man who appeared to be the father of her children. He had dark features that were evident in the faces of all three kids. He wondered about this man but knew it was not his place to ask.

He ordered a variety of sushi since Alyce had no idea what she would like. She seemed content to let him order everything, and Ben was happy to do so. When the food arrived, he noticed that she paused, so he asked if she'd mind him asking a blessing. Her eyes once again lit up as she instinctively reached across the table for his hand and bowed her head. They held hands and prayed as if it were their regular habit.

When he said amen, he heard her echoed reply. Looking up, slight tears glistened in her eyes.

"Thank you for that," Alyce said. She closed her eyes briefly and drew in a deep breath. When she opened them, she grabbed her chopsticks and said, "Now, show me how this is done!" They laughed as she maneuvered awkwardly.

"I read somewhere that the use of chopsticks is an American thing," Ben said as he laid his aside. "The Japanese eat with their fingers." At that, he selected a piece and popped it in his mouth. Alyce followed suit, and they soon made quick work of their meal.

Dinner was pleasant, and the two were surprised when they realized almost every other table had emptied. They gathered their things and walked down beside the pool. Laughter carried up from the beach on a breeze that cooled the air. Alyce untied a scarf from her bag and wrapped it around her shoulders. She stood in the light reflecting from the pool as palm trees swayed behind her. Ben said a prayer that, whatever had led Alyce to a vacation by herself, she realized how special she was.

"What?" Alyce asked, breaking his reverie.

Ben smiled and attempted to deflect from the fact that he was again guilty of staring at her. "You should have your picture made!"

"Don't be silly," Alyce said demurely. She paused and then added, "But wait! I *do* want you to take my picture."

Alyce produced her phone and, setting the camera, handed it to Ben. She struck a pose like she'd seen her girls do in countless shots, and Ben snapped several, including one up close. Looking to make sure he'd gotten good ones, Ben suddenly had an idea.

"Wait here and let me grab something from my car," he said as he backed away. "I'll be right back."

Alyce walked to the pool railing and scrolled through the pictures. She wanted to send one to the kids so they'd see she was having a great time. When he reappeared, he was carrying his camera. "Do you mind?" he asked hesitantly, halfway lifting the camera to his eye as he gestured. Ben realized she might find having her picture made by someone she'd only just met incredibly awkward.

Over dinner they had discussed Lillian's upcoming senior exhibit and her daughter's passion for photography. Alyce had been her daughter's model since she'd gotten her first disposable camera. So, although at first Alyce was hesitant, soon she relaxed, and Ben snapped away. She assumed the role of subject as Ben got caught up in his hobby and the beautiful night. Alyce appeared carefree and smiled a brilliant smile as she goofed around, leaning on the pool chaise, tossing her hair into the breeze.

Ben held the camera down and scrolled through the photos he'd taken. Alyce was pretty, but beyond that, an inner light seemed to shine through her eyes. He felt she'd be shocked by her own visage. He showed her a few, but Alyce was not prepared to see herself with the changes she'd made to her appearance. It was all too much: the makeover, dinner with a strange man. Turning away, she sat gently on the edge of the chaise. In a matter of seconds, she was in tears, her shoulders shaking as she wept.

With no preparation for this response, Ben did what any person would have done. He quickly sat beside her and put his arm around her shoulders to console her as best he could, awkwardly trying not to violate her personal space. His heart was torn for his new friend. He could do nothing but sit close and be present.

"Shhhh," Ben said as he patted her arm. Alyce tucked her hair behind her ear. His mother had taught him to always carry a handkerchief, which he now offered. At first she was stiff at his attempts, but she finally laid her head over on his shoulder and cried silently. They sat in stillness until her sniffs diminished. He almost didn't hear her when she finally spoke.

"Now I can't breathe through my nose."

He leaned back and looked at her. Her eyes were puffy, her face splotchy, and her nose bright red from crying. But she had a mock-serious look that made him burst out laughing. This woman was too much.

She gently took the camera from his hands and began scrolling through the photos. Ben stood and grabbed a chair, pulling it close enough to view the pictures with Alyce. "Me thinks thou needest a good cry," Ben spoofed. He knew the value of releasing pent-up emotions.

"I do apologize for snotting all over you," Alyce said as she stood to go. She returned his camera to him. "I think it's time for me to head inside."

Ben understood. He suspected that she'd only checked her emotions until she could be safely alone. Then the floodgates would open, and it would not be a pretty cry. He would let her go, but he had to admit he liked the way she felt in his arms. They had more time tomorrow and the next day before he had to head back to Birmingham. He smiled at the thought of finding out more about this intriguing woman.

"Sweet dreams," Alyce tossed over her shoulder as she gathered her small bag and the beautiful peonies Ben had brought her. "I love these!" she called to him as she walked away.

"Until tomorrow?" Ben queried.

"You'll know where to find me!" And with that, Alyce slipped away into the darkness.

Ben couldn't remember when he'd felt this way. He'd abused women so tragically over the years before Christ. Since then, he'd not even entertained the thought of another woman in his life except for business. Maybe it was time to safely wade into the dating waters again. Maybe…

Chapter Eight
MICHAEL

ichael pulled his little sports car into the driveway of the place that had been home for the past twenty-two years. He could see a lamp burning inside, but otherwise, the place was dark. After Maggie had left the office, he'd lost his mojo for work and had no intention of engaging the gathering in the conference room.

After he left, he'd called back to the office and sent Carrie home early to her husband, who was on spring break for the week and, therefore, had some flexibility with his evenings. Michael encouraged her to treat him to dinner somewhere and offered to call a couple of different spots to secure the two of them a reservation. But she had declined, saying they had strung lights on their back patio over the weekend and were going to grill and have a candlelight dinner outside.

He could remember those days. Young and in love. Not needing any bells or whistles to make life exciting. Blissfully content in each other's presence.

Most of the afternoon, he had driven around. Though he'd tried the past few months to replace old memories by taking Cassidy to his favorite spots, most places he drove past only reminded him of Alyce— or at least the Alyce he knew. Good old predictable Alyce was proving not so predictable.

Now he sat in the driveway looking at the dear old house. Alyce had pined for it but never begged or pleaded. One thing for sure, Alyce wasn't a whiner.

He thought about the voicemail he'd just heard from Cassidy. For some reason, her normally provocative tone had seemed annoying as all get out. He didn't fully even hear what she'd said. Something about how bored she was and didn't he want to go clubbing tonight?

She completely lost him at that suggestion. He had never developed a taste for the club scene, although he'd done his share of it in college. Cassidy knew he didn't enjoy it, so why the devil did she think he'd want to go tonight?

He had tried going with her once, before Alyce knew all that was going on between the two of them. He'd sat alone at a table while Cassidy danced with some of her girlfriends, occasionally waving to him from the dance floor. Why had he found that so intoxicating at the time? Now, clubbing was the last thing on his agenda for that night or any night.

Besides, he was not pleased with her. She had taken the entire day for her "doctor's appointment." He felt certain she had no such appointment. More likely, she was getting her hair and nails done, the first such liberty she'd taken since they'd been together. Somehow, he knew it wouldn't be the last.

He pulled the car around to his usual spot in the back of the house, causing the motion-sensor lights to turn on. Anytime he'd come by since he moved out, he had used the front door and rarely made it past the porch. Alyce made sure he stayed outside unless it was unavoidable. He thought it might feel awkward coming there tonight, but it seemed natural and easy, like seeing an old friend. He was surprised at how the tension seemed to ease as he parked and got out of the car.

Placing his key in the lock, he was shocked to find it wouldn't work. Had Alyce changed them? He remembered they had always hidden one behind a loose rock in the facade of the patio. He took a chance, reaching into the hole that had been their convenient hiding place all these years. Sure enough; the shiny, new key was right where he'd expected. More surprises from not-so-predictable Alyce: changing the locks on the doors.

As he pushed open the door, the *beep, beep, beep* of the alarm system that greeted him caused him to freeze. What if she'd changed the code to that, too? He punched in the six digits he'd used for the ten years they'd had the system. It continued to beep a warning sound. Pulling out his readers, he propped them on his nose and peered at the screen. "Please enter correct passcode." Dang it! What was up with that woman anyway? Why was she changing everything?

He didn't have long to act. Quickly, he called Maggie to secure the password and whatever else he might need for the security people when they called. As he dialed, he braced himself for the blaring alarm to begin at any minute. Sure enough, about the time Maggie answered, her voice was drowned out by the blaring siren. He knew shortly the house phone would ring, and it would be the alarm company asking the important questions.

"Hello?" Michael plugged one ear with his finger and stood poised to punch in the numbers with his other. The horns continued to blow. "Hello, Maggie?"

To his surprise, Jackson answered Maggie's phone. "Mr. Keriman?" he replied. "Sir, where are you?" he asked in response to the horrific sounds competing with his father-in-law's voice.

"I'm at the house," Michael shouted into the phone. "I don't know the alarm code."

He heard Jackson shouting to Maggie, "Hey, babe, your dad's at your mom's house, and he doesn't know the alarm code!" That stung a little, but in that moment, Michael couldn't care.

"She wants to know what you're doing at the house," Jackson relayed.

"I needed to get a few things, but that doesn't matter! I still pay for this house, and I need that code now!" he snapped into the phone.

"Yes, sir!" Jackson replied, like a private responding to a general. Michael heard muffled talking and then a hurried, "It's 252218, sir."

Michael had barely entered the digits when the house phone began ringing. In all their years living there, the only times the alarm had been triggered was on accident by one of them. Except once, when a storm with strong winds rattled the doors and windows, setting it screaming in the middle of the night. Thankful that the noise had ceased, he grabbed the house phone and quickly answered the security questions. Thank goodness those hadn't changed!

Finally, all was quiet—except he kept hearing a voice. It sounded like someone talking far away. Suddenly, Michael realized he had never ended his call with Jackson. He was still waiting on the phone and calling out to him to get his attention. He put it back to his ear.

"Jackson! Son, I'm sorry; I forgot about you."

"That's no problem, sir. Quite understandable."

"And I'm sorry I snapped at you. Rough day."

"Understood."

"You doing alright?"

"Yes, sir. Maggie isn't feeling so great, but I'm taking care of her."

"Then carry on, son," Michael said as he hung up the phone.

He flipped on the kitchen light, remembering to step over the loose floor tile he had been meaning to repair for over three years now. To his surprise, the tile was fixed. He wondered who Alyce had gotten to do the work and how much it had cost him. He could have done it if she'd just waited. Michael smiled to himself as he realized the irony of his thoughts.

Little things seemed different as he moved about the house. At first, he thought he'd just been unobservant all those years. Maybe that candle had always been there? And those oversized pillows stacked on the floor? The more he observed, however, the more he realized that furniture had definitely been rearranged and items added to the decor.

He felt like an investigator searching for clues. As he mounted the bottom stair to continue his inspection, he glanced into the dining room and saw fabric swatches scattered amongst paint samples and photos from magazines. Maybe she was going to redecorate. Surely she wasn't preparing to sell the place! It was home.

Suddenly a strong urge propelled him straight up the stairs, two at a time, and into their bedroom. He knew before turning on the light to expect changes as Alyce had spent countless hours trying to convince him they needed to redo their room.

"It should be a haven for us," she'd say.

He didn't like the thought of having to sleep in Maggie's old room while the work was being done. He liked his own bed. And besides, why did they need a fancy bedroom anyway? All they did was sleep there. The slightest ping of guilt pinched his conscience at those thoughts.

Standing there now, he had to admit the room before him was beautiful. Alyce was a talented decorator. Her designs were fresh and welcoming. Everyone described their home as nurturing, and the two of them had entertained many souls there over the years.

Now their bedroom had been transformed with soothing, cool colors in direct contrast to the dated red and gold pattern from before.

He'd helped select the bold comforter over ten years before and couldn't see why they needed a new one. The old, faded rug had been replaced with a luxurious, muted pattern of gray and ivory. He slipped off his shoes and sank his feet into its softness.

Looking at their bed, he thought he recognized the old headboard, but Alyce had painted it, and now, against the new wall color, it seemed more elegant than before. A pile of plush pillows was arranged at the head of the bed, with the central one bearing a message: "I am my Beloved's." Michael recognized the familiar passage from the Song of Solomon in the Bible. He wondered at its meaning for Alyce since they had been separated for nine months now. He wanted to stretch out on the bed to see if it yielded its familiar softness but thought better of it.

Opening the bathroom door, he switched on the light and stepped from tranquility into chaos. Most of the wallpaper had been stripped, and there were rolls of new, waiting to be hung. A small, crystal chandelier he vaguely remembered Alyce purchasing several years back now hung over the bathtub. The shower tiles had been replaced with gorgeous Carrara marble, and the new plumbing fixtures everywhere sparkled in the light from the chandelier.

Several thoughts struck Michael at once. First, this was clearly beautiful work done primarily by his wife. He had forgotten how talented she was. Second, he wasn't quite sure where she'd gotten her money to make the purchases. Oddly, it didn't really bother him. He was enjoying the changes he found. He had to admit this was much better than the same old way it had been. But he also knew no sign of this activity had shown up on their bank account.

He remembered the collection on the dining table and darted back downstairs to see what she had planned next. To his amazement, she had neatly organized files with notes that indicated she'd been planning to redo the house since the beginning of Harrison's senior year. It even appeared she wanted her own office space.

He wondered why she needed an entire room for her stuff. To him, the entire house was hers. As he flipped through the file, he saw she was planning a space designated to keep her books and journals and all those crafting supplies she'd bought over the years. On one sticky note she had written in bold letters, "NEED A SPACE WITH A DOOR/LOCK!!!" Now he recalled that she'd often said how much she'd enjoy having a room where things could be left out and easily accessible, one with a door so she could quickly shut out the noise or hide the mess, whichever the occasion might demand.

She had pictures of open-concept kitchens and family areas that were beautiful. How many times had she asked to tear down the wall between the kitchen and den to do this project? She hated that it separated them all during the evenings as he sat reading the paper while the kids watched TV and she was busy in the kitchen.

When Maggie was a freshman in college, she happened to be home one weekend as Alyce was once again broaching the subject of tearing down the wall.

"You sound like Ronald Reagan!" he'd griped. "Tear down that wall!"

Maggie had casually commented that the wall seemed symbolic of her parents' life: always together but often not in the same space. Michael would admit that as much as they loved and enjoyed each other, as the years progressed, something always seemed to stand between them. Based on her drawings and scribbles, he could now totally see how great it would be to open up the floor plan. He wondered what their home might be like if he gave Alyce carte blanche to do whatever was necessary to bring it to its full potential.

He picked up a folder marked "Nursery." At first, resentment rose to the top of his emotions, assuming she'd already known Maggie and Jackson's news before she left for wherever she was. But scribbled on the front of the folder was a date from two years prior and the word "Someday." Michael realized that Alyce was just preparing for what might come as she dreamed and planned for their future after the children had gone.

The contents of the folder blurred slightly. Tears filled Michael's eyes as he combed over his findings. There were three 5x7 black-and-white photos, one of each of their children clipped together. Each child appeared to be around two years old. A sticky note on the back read, "Enlarge on canvas." He remembered Maggie saying her mom was planning to transform her old room into the nursery. He couldn't wait to see the finished project, then realized he might never have the opportunity.

Michael walked to the kitchen fridge. He was hopeful for some of Alyce's yummy leftovers. Her cooking was great when hot, but he confessed he liked it just as well cold. He had never seen the refrigerator so empty. He remembered she wouldn't have left anything perishable while she was away.

One of her quirks he loved was that everything had to be in perfect shape before they could ever go out of town. The dishwasher must be run and clean dishes put away. No clothes or toys could be left lying around. Beds were made and sofa pillows fluffed. Trash cans were emptied and contents taken outside.

One day, early in their marriage, Michael had asked Alyce why everything had to be so clean before they could leave. Was *Southern Living* coming by for a photo shoot?

"What if something happens to us, God forbid, and our loved ones have to come here for our funeral? I don't want them finding all our trash or thinking that we live like…that we live…" Alyce struggled to find the right word.

"Here?" Michael offered, to which Alyce just huffed, causing him to burst out laughing. He had seldom thought beyond packing a simple bag before getting on the road. However, through her influence over the years, he had developed his own "pre-trip" routine that included making sure all the kids' outside toys were in the garage and the hose was neatly coiled and put away. He policed the outside because he knew she was vigilant about the inside.

Michael closed the refrigerator door. All he'd wanted was a cold drink and a piece of fried chicken. Instead, there he stood reminiscing again. Perhaps coming here had not been such a good idea. He couldn't really remember what prompted him to come in the first place. When he left the office, he'd turned onto the interstate instead of heading to his condo in the Gulch. Odd, as his autopilot setting of heading home should have been overridden by the new routine by now.

A light was blinking on the answering machine. Should he listen? He desperately wanted to do so. Not because he was nosy but because listening is what he would routinely do if this were still his home. Most likely, the message was something he'd delete, a solicitation or telemarketer.

Neither of them liked the blinking light. Nor did they like the little red circles on their cell phones, indicating there were unread messages, texts, or calls there. Michael smiled at the myriad of times one of them had lamented over some new app on their phone that created even more red circles. He wasn't a fan of change or learning new things, but many of the changes did seem to make life simpler.

His own phone had become an albatross around his neck. It wore him out, the constant accessibility to whomever needed him. The varying sounds and vibrations seemed incessant at times. And, oh, the money he had exhausted trying to improve the internet speed at their house. Alyce had said it didn't really bother her when texts were delayed or calls dropped. The kids knew they could reach their parents on the landline. The ones who needed to access them most could reach them old-school style.

He decided it best to leave the light for Alyce to find when she got home. A few pieces of mail were scattered on the counter beside the phone. This would have never been the work of Alyce. Everything had to be in its place before she would leave town. One of the kiddos must have dropped by and brought in the mail. Did that mean she was planning to be gone a long time?

Michael grabbed each piece and neatly arranged them smallest to largest. When he went to tuck them into the organizer on the kitchen desk, he noticed the "family" calendar hanging and couldn't help but peruse it. At first he thought Alyce had abandoned her routine of using a different color marker for each family member, but then it hit him that they knew less and less of their children's comings and goings.

How long had they planned for this day? The empty nest and a return to just the two of them? As his practice had grown, so too had their children, and the bigger the children, the more they seemed to cost. But they had a long-range plan for the day their children would be independent, and the money he earned could be spent on themselves.

By the time Harrison graduated college, the girls would be through school and potentially married with jobs. He and Alyce were going to travel and enjoy day trips, sometimes taking off in the middle of an afternoon, just because they could. They'd drive or they'd fly. They'd be gone overnight or for two weeks at a time. They'd go to long-dreamed-about destinations and experience new places she'd read about in a magazine. As long as they were together, they would tackle any adventure. It would be fun!

"I do think it might have been fun."

Michael realized he'd spoken out loud into the vastness of the empty house. He looked around at the comfort and familiarity, even in the subtle changes. What was wrong with him? "It must be the revelation that I am going to be a grandfather," he again spoke out loud. Forcefully, another thought crashed into his psyche, *You left all of this for a reason. Get out now before you try to move back in!*

He turned on his heel and made a beeline for his car, careful to return the key to its hiding place after locking the door. Halfway to the interstate, he realized he'd forgotten to set the alarm. Dang it! He turned his car around in the nearest parking lot, but in the frenzy, he wheeled around without looking. He heard the horn and the crunch of metal before it even registered he'd pulled into the path of another car.

He got out and walked around to view the damage, fortunately minimal as neither party had much speed. His frustration mounted, and he quickly swapped info with the other driver. Why had he thought it was a good idea to go to the house? The past two days had been overwhelming disasters. And all he could think about was his wife sitting on the beach.

Chapter Nine

ALYCE

*B*efore Alyce could open her eyes, the brilliant sun was already blinding. Her head pounded, and she knew that opening her peepers would only increase the pain. Why was it so bright in her bedroom?

She slid from the bed, never opening her eyes, and stumbled to the bathroom for some pain meds. Safely inside the windowless room, she allowed herself to peek through narrow slits at her reflection in the mirror. Her eyes were swollen and sore. Behind her she could see through the open door that the drapes on the large, floor-to-ceiling windows were wide open. Ordinarily, Alyce would have closed them before going to bed. Seeing them caused her to unpack the events of the previous night, starting with her outburst with Ben at the pool.

She had made it back to the condo and, once safely inside, allowed months of pent-up emotion to flow. All the grief she'd carried over what appeared to be the death of her dreams flowed like the Cumberland River. All the negativity and self-shaming she'd allowed into her spirit rushed out as she thought of every time she'd gotten her hopes up for Michael to come home, only to have them dashed again and again. Feeling like such a mistake of a wife one minute, then suppressing extreme anger at her husband the next.

She sorted through her feelings, scattered about like the folders of samples and clippings on her dining room table at home. Each one told her something different about herself, much of it unkind. What she longed for most in that moment was the ability to keep the folders that were simple and life giving and discard the ones that brought chaos into her spirit and into her life.

She found the ibuprofen and opened it, shaking the pills into her hand. Just before she tossed them into her mouth, she turned on a light to be certain she had found the right bottle. Assured in the light, she turned toward the sink to fill a glass with water and caught a glimpse of herself in the mirror.

Though still jarring to see her new haircut and color, Alyce felt good about the woman looking back at her, puffy eyes and all. Last night, totally spent from the energy she'd expelled in tears, she'd only managed to remove her clothes and slip into a sleep shirt before collapsing into bed. Now she bore the signs of leftover makeup, a pillow-creased impression on her cheek, and those pitiful little pillows under her eyes.

Turning on the hot water, she let it warm while she took a cotton pad and dotted it with eye makeup remover. Though not much mascara was left, a few swipes removed every trace. She lathered her face with cleanser then took the warm, wet washcloth and wiped away the remnants of yesterday. It felt good as she rinsed the washcloth and covered her face again, allowing the warmth to ease the strain she felt through her eyes.

Moisturizer was next. Alyce smoothed it over her face and neck, then dotted eye cream around her eyes.

Could someone please just bring in a giant cloth and wipe away everything to help me transition from this season of life to the next? she thought. How in the world does anyone get on with life when they feel as if their entire past has been a farce? Would that there were some crazy invention to destroy every trace of bad memories and sorrow from the past year.

She had been writing her life's story with a specific set of characters for a long time. Now, not only was her husband writing himself out of the story, but her daughters were both in a segue. And Harrison, well, he hadn't needed his mom in a long time, although she knew he loved her dearly. His role in this story was more and more that of a guest appearance.

While it had been the intention all along for the children to evolve, she had not held that expectation for Michael. How very cruel of him to establish such a fake sense of permanence in her story and then walk away as if he were trading a used car.

She felt a new wave of fury rising. What did he know anyway? He'd never had any taste apart from her. Why, he wouldn't even know how to dress and appreciate the finer things in life without her influence. Who was he fooling to think that he was going to be able to do life without her? He was a selfish, pompous jackass! That was precisely what he was!

Alyce had never been one to call names. At first, she balked and scolded herself for using such an unladylike word. But looking at her puffy face in the mirror, she stepped back and addressed herself there. "He *is* a jackass! He is a first-class, number-one, highly competent jackass!" She looked around the room. No one had heard her. Who was she hurting?

"I *am* sorry, Lord," she confessed, rather sheepishly. "I know he's Your child and You love him, but that felt *soooo* good! How do You tolerate him? Oh, my gosh! Can You even believe him?" She laughed at the thought of sharing a conversation with God about calling her husband a jackass.

Walking back into the bedroom, she stood at the end of the bed and allowed herself to fall backward into the jumble of covers. She stretched a long, luxurious stretch. Then she stood up and did a few squats, arms extended straight in front of her, just because it felt good. Her mind was gloriously empty for the first time in months.

The night before, she had confronted massive amounts of ugliness in her spirit, the process gross and painful like an abscess that had been opened and cleaned out. Sadly, she had no magic washcloth to clean away the refuse. The process was, by necessity, excruciating, but she would embrace the pain if it brought her closer to her true self, the one God planned when He created her. She'd not seen that girl in a long time.

Every morning, day after day since she'd learned of Michael's infidelity, Alyce had awakened to the same heaviness. Her mind was crowded with every possible ounce of hurt it could contain. Like a mass of energy, the thoughts were restless and stayed in constant motion every moment of the day until she collapsed into bed each night. But right now, as her headache eased, she found herself almost confounded because she couldn't even decide what to think. None of the heaviness lingered. She felt free, like a bird that had forgotten it could fly and had just leapt from the nest for the first time in years.

Suddenly, her stomach reminded her that she could not take medicine without food. She raced to the kitchen and found a box of crackers, quickly munching a few, then retired to her chair by the glass doors to sit quietly while they settled her stomach.

Alyce thought about Ben. It felt odd and right at the same time. He was kind and gentle. He had told her how beautiful she looked. Was it her imagination, or had he genuinely seemed delighted at the "new"

Alyce? Not that he'd ever known the old one. But his reaction to her communicated much about what he saw. Today, the new Alyce chose to believe he found her pretty.

She closed her eyes and sat quietly, replaying their conversation in her mind. She smelled something sweet and turned to look at the peonies on the table beside her.

Flowers! How long had it been since anyone had sent her flowers? And not just any flowers but her favorite flowers! Alyce knew he had taken great care in selecting something for her. Ben had done his homework.

Alyce wanted peonies in her wedding bouquet, but she also wanted to marry in December, when peonies cost an arm and a leg. She had dreamed of a Christmas wedding since she was a girl. December also coordinated with Michael's winter break at school. Peonies were far too expensive for their families to afford in the off season.

She thought about the beautiful bouquet of red roses and ivy she had carried on that unseasonably warm day. They were gorgeous. Everything about Alyce and Michael's wedding had been. She had no regrets...*except maybe the person you married?*

Where did that come from? she wondered. It felt good to be free from the negative thoughts about herself. Alyce would purpose in her heart not to swap one set of negatives for another.

Wonder what he's doing? I wonder if he even knows I've left town. If he does, I can't imagine he much cares. Let's see; it's Tuesday. I think the sixteenth? He should be headed into the office about now. I hope he remembers it's his sister's birthday. I should remind him.

Alyce instinctively reached for her phone, then stopped herself. It was going to take some time and would definitely require reprogramming her everyday life, but she was not his partner any longer. He would have to figure it all out for himself.

She would not be the one left with regret when the dust settled and all that remained of their marriage were three beautiful children and whatever future grandbabies they might produce. She would not allow herself to be bitter. That was the one character trait she'd witnessed in too many of her divorced friends. Bitterness was the least attractive accessory one could wear, and she realized she had far too much gratitude in her heart to surrender any ground to bitterness.

Maybe Michael had done her a favor. Maybe a chance at a do-over was something every woman secretly dreamed of in her life. *She* certainly hadn't done anything to contribute to his poor choices. *Had she?*

Alyce sat up straighter and gazed out to where the azure water met the clear, blue sky. As it sparkled and danced, she imagined her heavenly Father standing atop the gently swelling waves. His hands were extended, and He was reaching for her. He seemed patient and kind. She sensed Him telling her to trust Him for more—for something out where she'd never thought of going. She wondered if she was bold enough to go to Him. Sure, she could stay safely in the shallows and wave and smile. He'd be okay with that. But she was going to miss something He alone could show her in the deep.

She closed her eyes and covered her face with her hands, massaging her forehead and opening her daily dialogue with the one she knew was incapable of being unfaithful, the one who loved her with an everlasting love she could never fully deserve. And yet, His approval alone made her worthy. As she greeted Him, she saw herself stepping toward the water's edge. Something deep and small and hidden swelled within her. Alyce inhaled sharply and slowly exhaled as she mentally felt the cool liquid of her first steps toward Him beneath her feet.

"Father, my brother Michael is deceived. Will You help me see him the way You see him? I don't understand his ways, and I certainly don't have a single answer. You do. You are the answer. I know You can teach me how to love him well. Lord, I pray that, starting right now, You will draw Michael back to You. If he never comes home to me, will You create in him a clean heart and renew his spirit to be right with You? His children, especially Harrison, need him to be a man of God. I can't make that happen, but I know You can. Will You keep corrupt companions far from him? Draw him to You as only You can. Remove the distractions and demands that keep him from hearing Your still, small voice. And bless us all this day to find peace. Amen."

Chapter Ten

BEN

*T*he past two days had flown by. Ben felt good. He and Alyce had spent many hours together—mostly laughing—since they'd officially met.

He'd never been around anyone quite like Alyce. Maybe their age made them so free from pretense and questionable agendas. Without playing games, they simply talked and talked for hours on end. They had started each of the past two days together on the beach. Then they'd moved to the poolside grill for lunch before returning to their chairs where they'd lingered into the evening.

The previous night, they had agreed to walk down the beach for dinner at a small, casual pizza place with outdoor seating. He appreciated the ease with which Alyce had put on a baseball cap and cover-up and strolled with him along the water's edge to grab a bite.

But tonight she had agreed to let him treat her to some place special. Ben had been coming to this area of Alabama since he was a boy. Sadly, too many of the nicer restaurants knew him because of the variety of women he had brought over the years. He was thankful he'd discovered a new place where the food was amazing, they knew him well, and they were always willing to free a table for him. Tonight he would take Alyce there.

This day had begun just like yesterday. Ben and Alyce had set up camp in their chairs on the beach under the big, blue umbrella. She quizzed him about Flannery O'Connor. They debated which was better, eighties bands or the big names like Diana Ross and Stevie Wonder. They agreed that jazz was the best, but New Orleans jazz took the prize.

When the time came for them to go inside, he could tell she hated missing their final sunset together. He promised that the place they were going had a view that would take her breath away. She'd reluctantly waited until the last possible moment to go in and get ready.

Now he stood in the bathroom with a towel wrapped around his waist, curls dripping from a long, hot shower. Using the side of his fist, he wiped a clear spot in the mirror and stared at himself. He was a handsome man, and it had been to his advantage. Of course, as a boy, he'd taken more than his share of teasing over his curls, but as he grew older, he used his appearance to make a way for himself.

In high school, he'd flirted shamelessly with the female teachers, just enough to be adorable and earn himself a few extra points or an extension on his term paper. His coaches didn't care a whit about his curls. He'd worked hard to earn his spot as tight end and had lettered sophomore, junior, and senior years. Consequently, Ben learned how to play everything to his advantage. Where looks couldn't win, his work ethic would.

College is where he realized his looks could garner other benefits. It initially startled him, the ease with which he could sleep with a coed without any thought beyond the random encounter. He had not been raised around promiscuity, but he had discovered his father's stack of porn around the age of ten. His perspective on women was a skewed mess between what he saw in the pages of those magazines and his mother, a beautiful, kind woman.

Oddly, his parents seemed to have a great relationship. He was confused by what his dad said and did with his mother and his hidden obsession with viewing other women in such a degrading manner. His dad treated his mom like a queen and insisted that Ben respect her always.

Ben viewed pornography increasingly over the years. He met and married his wife, Amie, in graduate school. She was stunning and also brilliant. Once, before they married, she discovered his stack of lewd magazines. She had broken off their engagement and told him he had no chance of marrying her while that issue lingered in his life.

He was shocked. He had no idea that it would be a problem. Although he and his dad never spoke of his pornography addiction, to him, this was normal. If his mother knew about his father's little secret, Ben would be surprised. She rarely visited the office where his dad kept the magazines in an old briefcase under his desk. His father was a successful attorney, and his office was cluttered with stacks of files and documents. If Mom did drop by, she avoided his desk and its chaotic arrangement for fear of upsetting something important.

Ben discovered the magazines one day while at the office. His mom had gone to be with his grandmother, who was recuperating from surgery. Ben's dad had a meeting he couldn't cancel, so he picked his son up from school and deposited him at his desk to do homework. Left to his own devices, Ben avoided the homework. He imagined what it would feel like to be powerful as he spun around and around in the huge chair. He fell to the floor, his head swimming.

That's when he saw it: the old, leather briefcase his dad carried sometimes on business trips. Not really a briefcase, more like a satchel, the two buckles on the front flaps were open. Ben peered inside, and finding it only contained a few magazines, he thought at first he'd simply push it back in place. But something drew him to look further.

The images he saw were at first shocking, then intriguing, then shaming. Mesmerized, Ben slowly turned the pages and gawked at the pictures of women who were scantily clad, then some with no clothes at all. He recognized one of the women from a show his family watched together on TV. He hadn't understood the feelings they aroused. In a rush of panic, he quickly replaced the magazines.

Thereafter, Ben discovered that several of his friends' dads hid the same magazines, some not very well. Around age thirteen, one dad began handing his off to his son, which his group of buddies arranged to swap among themselves. As time passed, Ben would vacillate between little concern for his behavior and the strong conviction that this was wrong. He longed to have a woman like his mother to love and share life with.

Maybe that was the answer. His father led a double life and got away with it. Why couldn't he? When Amie almost walked away from their engagement, he stopped looking at pornography. He truly loved her—or at least the idea of her. That someone so smart and beautiful could be his wife made him despise the weakness of allowing something immaterial to jeopardize their future. Besides, his dad was proof he could juggle both if it came down to it. He avoided the temptation for five years.

While on a business trip, Ben found himself with free time and turned on the TV in his hotel room. The opening menu advertised Adult Viewing. That was all it took. He fell immediately into old habits that gradually led to numerous affairs, one-night stands, and eventually the demise of his marriage.

Through an inpatient facility for sexual addictions, he had been radically changed. The process required him to face his demons head-on. He certainly couldn't change on his own. It took some incredible people in his life, and, in fairness, he was still a work in progress. But fully embracing a life and relationship with Jesus Christ was the only way he could now tolerate himself.

He wished he could take it back. Oh, how he wished he could take it back. Amie had been gracious to him the first time she learned of his affairs. He really couldn't fault her for refusing to even consider forgiveness the second time, especially after the doctor's diagnosis. Who could blame her? Certainly not Ben. He'd spent countless hours since his transformation replaying what might have been, if only.

By the time he had adopted God's agenda, rather than asking God to bless the one he had composed, Amie had remarried. She was now living in Atlanta with their two beautiful children. Ben's son and daughter were in high school and being raised by another man.

Even so, he possessed peace in his life he couldn't quite articulate. Truthfully, there had been bitterness with God over the way things had transpired. But, if Ben were honest with himself, the life he now lived had been built with his own hands. He could ask why me all he wanted, but the answer would always come back around to his choices. He could have followed a different path than that of his father's. He could have chosen integrity and surrendered that part of himself, but he hadn't. And while what was done could not be undone, it could be forgiven. It *had* been forgiven—by God and by Amie. For that, Ben felt immense joy and gratitude and peace.

The kids were coming around to the idea of a relationship, particularly his son. Amie noticed the change in Ben before he ever said a word, and she was glad. She had never stopped praying for him and was likely the reason he was where he was today. He loved her dearly for her abiding confidence in God's ability to work a miracle in his life. But he knew that their love would forever be different because she now belonged to another man.

His phone beeped, startling him back to reality. A brief text from Alyce read, "Are you sure about the sunset at this place? Have you looked outside to see how dazzling the water looks right now? You're taking me away from something incredible..."

He knew she was teasing. Seeing a text from her made his heart feel odd in his chest as he realized they might part ways tomorrow and never see each other again. Birmingham and Nashville weren't that far apart, but he knew little about her life there. She had told him about her three children, and their lives seemed intertwined, even though they were all three practically grown. With a new grandbaby on the way, she wouldn't likely have time for visits from him, much less time to head south to Birmingham.

He sent back, "I promise! Trust me," and continued getting ready for the evening. Whatever the night held for them, he was going to make it beautiful and memorable. He would be respectful and treat Alyce the way he should have treated Amie. He wasn't sure what her story was regarding an ex-husband, but perhaps dinner would be when he found out.

Ben shaved and brushed his teeth before stepping into the bedroom to cool off a moment before dressing. He knelt at the foot of the bed, the best posture for him to pray.

"Father, I can't ever come to You without first saying thank You for rearranging my life. You are vigilant and faithful, despite my unfaithfulness to You. I don't know what this night holds for me and Alyce, but I pray that when it's done, we'll both feel we've honored You through our words and our deeds. Thank You for my new friend. I pray You'll bless her as she returns home, and, if it's part of Your plan, I'd love to stay friends for a long time. You give incredible gifts. Amen."

Chapter Eleven
ALYCE

*W*hy did Alyce feel so jittery inside? There was nothing about her relationship with Ben that had been remotely inappropriate. Was that it? Was she afraid he might try to kiss her and she would have to shut him down? Or maybe she was afraid she wouldn't want to shut him down. And everything within Alyce knew that a kiss would be the same thing as what Michael had done to her.

Well, no, her psyche interrupted. *It wouldn't be quite the same.*

Alyce was uncomfortable with that thought. Unfaithfulness was unfaithfulness, no matter what definition society put on it. Michael was still her husband. At least on paper. And in God's eyes? Maybe she should cancel dinner. What if he thought it was a date? She didn't know what to do.

Alyce, she scolded herself, *you are two adult friends going to dinner. Your intentions are pure and you will correct his if the need arises.* She should have felt better, but there lingered a heavy foreboding. She brushed it aside as she brushed her hair.

There was the matter of what to wear. If Alyce were completely honest, a part of her felt rebellious and wanted to pretend she *was* going on a date. It was as close as she'd ever come to paying Michael back for all he'd done. Couldn't she have just that little bit of satisfaction? A simple date before they were officially divorced? Although he'd likely never know and for certain wouldn't care, she liked to imagine his face if he learned she'd done something so out of character. She hated being predictable. Maybe tonight was her chance to be unpredictable.

When she'd packed for this trip, she was in a very low place and only threw in swimsuits, cover-ups, and casual shorts outfits. She hadn't banked on two nice dinners with anyone, let alone a man.

She purchased a dress for their sushi meal in the little boutique inside the salon. It was simple and a beautiful aquamarine, like the ocean. Ben had complimented her on the way it brought out her blue eyes. When she'd bought it, she reasoned it was something she would wear again to dinner with friends, although it did show off her developing tan and her shoulders very nicely. Maybe there was a little more to it than just buying a nice dress. Maybe.

After pizza the night before, she'd excused herself by telling him she needed to call the girls. She had actually showered, then headed to the mall for a quick shopping excursion. Now she stood staring at two dresses laid out before her on the bed. She'd bought them both right as the announcement came that the store was closing. It was totally unlike her to be so spontaneous.

She picked up the first one, a black dress, and pulled it over her head. It was strapless, but tasteful. It had been a long time since she'd worn black, except to a funeral, and certainly nothing strapless. Actually, it had been a while since she'd worn anything at all that made her feel the slightest bit attractive. Michael hadn't noticed or commented in so long that she'd convinced herself she was too old and it was pointless. She liked that it was a maxi and the way her simple, diamond necklace shimmered on her skin.

Either dress would be complemented by her diamond hoop earrings, a guilt gift from Michael that she secretly loved. When he'd given them to her, she was so angry and hurt that she'd put them away and never worn them until now.

Michael had walked in from work with the earrings one evening. This was after she'd confronted him and he'd denied an affair—yet again. Now Alyce had hard evidence. She would settle for nothing less than admission of guilt and some sign of genuine repentance. Remorse was not the same as repentance and a gift was nothing if not accompanied by a sorrowful heart.

Still, that evening Alyce was in a pleasant mood and had hopes that their dinner could lead to genuine conversation. Michael stood rather impatiently at the end of the kitchen counter where she was preparing their small dinner.

"These are for you."

"What is this?"

She had to stop and dry her hands where she'd been chopping ingredients for a salad. The box was not wrapped as a gift. No sweet words of endearment or a kiss accompanied them. He just walked in the door, pulled the box from his briefcase, and flipped it open to reveal what should have been a beautiful gift. He slid them across to her as if he dreaded the thought of coming closer.

"It's something you always said you wanted," he'd deadpanned, shrugging his shoulders.

As Alyce wiped her hands and rounded the end of the counter, she noticed the earrings were set in white gold, while she typically wore yellow gold jewelry. The hoops were larger than her norm, but she liked them. For a moment, she wanted to gush over the extravagant gift. It was very uncharacteristic of Michael.

But when she reached out to touch them, it reminded her of the Wicked Witch of the West trying to touch Dorothy's ruby slippers. Her hand recoiled in disgust. Bile rose in her throat as her mind quickly readjusted.

In the past months there had been a volley of confrontation and denial between the two of them. During this time, she'd often felt like her brain was scrambled eggs with all of Michael's vehement rebuffs and ridiculous explanations for the facts she'd gathered confirming an affair. But now she was certain she wasn't insane. And like a Rubik's Cube when the last panel of matching colors falls into place, Alyce's thoughts had aligned with stunning clarity. The earrings were the last straw. She spoke venomously.

"What, your girlfriend didn't like them and you couldn't get your money back?"

Alyce was startled at how good it felt to be heartless and indifferent. Not one to be verbally quick witted, she didn't flinch when he snapped the box shut, tossed it on the counter, and quipped, "Take it or leave it. I bought them for you." She returned to her chopping with such a fervor that she almost cut her finger.

Such animosity was inconsistent with Alyce's nature. It took all she had not to apologize later as they ate their dinner in complete silence. The box sat on the counter for days until Alyce finally put it away in her jewelry drawer. She'd decide what to do with them, but not in the light of those circumstances.

As Alyce packed for the beach, she brought them along on a whim. A totally random force made her tuck the little blue box in her bag. The earrings hadn't been in her ears until that evening as she dressed for dinner with Ben. She decided that it was fitting to wear them as she went on what could be her "first date" as a free woman.

There, she admitted it. This felt like a date to her and for a moment she allowed herself to enjoy a little thrill. Which was quickly replaced with an onslaught of emotions, beginning with guilt, which was met by vindication, which was followed by the oddest sadness and longing in her innermost being. Alyce was not quite sure what tonight was supposed to be, but it surely resembled a date.

She felt as if she were finally surrendering her marriage to some giant, devouring beast that had hovered for the past two years, licking his chops and sharpening his knife. Slowly and quite patiently, he'd cut off a little of it here and a bigger chunk there, mocking Alyce by chewing slowly and deliberately right in front of her.

This analogy in her head was startling. She'd not recognized these feelings until now and wasn't sure what to do with them. Alyce was a gentle spirit, but she was not one to surrender without fighting tooth and nail for something in which she believed. She had always believed in her marriage. For a second time, she thought about calling Ben to cancel.

As she turned, she caught her reflection in the mirror and the light danced with the glimmer of the diamond earrings swinging gently from her ears. Her appearance surprised her. She looked healthy and whole. There was something else there, too. Alyce realized she actually looked happy.

She thought of each of her children and how they'd individually and collectively given her their blessing no matter what she chose to do about her marriage. She thought of Ben and his kind, encouraging words the past few days. The choices for their marriage, made by her husband on her behalf and without her acquiescence, were already done. This was a no-brainer. Alyce was going to dinner with Ben.

Slipping the black dress back over her head, she picked up the other, a white one. Simple and sleeveless, it fit her beautifully and came right to her knee. It was quite sassy and she didn't mind the way her legs looked in the strappy heels she'd snagged on her dash from the department store. What sort of signals would she be sending if she wore the white one?

Alyce's heart raced as she looked at the clock and realized there wasn't much time left. She removed the white dress and quickly painted her toenails in the final moments before she had to decide. She stood under the ceiling fan, praying that this would be her last hot flash of the night. Her mind was a jumble and she wished for one of her girls to give an opinion on which dress to choose. She almost laughed as she felt it quite ludicrous, the thought of one of her grown daughters helping choose a dress for a date.

Crossing into the bathroom, she outlined her lips, then filled them in with a neutral shade that would match either dress she chose to wear. She sprayed her perfume, then walked back to stand under the fan one more time. Breathing a prayer, she surveyed the two dresses before her.

A text beeped and she glanced down to read, "Your chariot awaits."

Confidently grabbing one of the dresses before her, she threw it on, slipped on her shoes, and ran to snag her purse. Passing through the kitchen, she opened the freezer door and leaned inside, the stark cold washing over her like a blessed balm. Mercy! Would she survive the evening? Even the thought of riding in a car together made her giddiness rise to extreme levels.

She still could not put her finger on this odd foreboding inside, so she chose to push it down into the reaches of her being and convince herself it was just nerves. The elevator ride down to the parking garage was barely enough time for one last pep talk.

As she emerged from the elevator, she was greeted by a long, low wolf whistle. Turning to her left, Ben strode toward her across the garage, hands in the pockets of his light, linen khakis. They were complemented by a white linen shirt, untucked, with the sleeves rolled twice. Her heart caught in her throat as she stood there facing a situation she'd never even dreamed would be a part of her life.

Ben extended his elbow and escorted her to the waiting vehicle, opening her door and politely standing aside as she slid onto the seat of his Range Rover. He'd already cranked the car and as he came around to get in, she quickly positioned the air vents to squelch the remains of any crazy sweating that remained. Taking a deep breath and exhaling just as he opened his door, Alyce was reminded of her mantra, "Exhale Alyce, inhale the Holy Spirit." She could do this. Ben was a friend and friends could go to dinner. Or was it a dinner date?

Alyce relaxed and breathed evenly as the car pulled onto the main road. *God hasn't given you a spirit of fear, Alyce,* she said to herself. She looked over at Ben and he smiled his dazzling smile. This was going to be fun. This wasn't a date, just dinner between friends. Dinner between two very groomed, immaculately dressed friends of the opposite sex, but friends nonetheless. So why was every nerve ending in Alyce's body on high alert?

Chapter Twelve
BEN AND ALYCE

*B*en wasn't kidding when he said the view of the sunset would be spectacular. They had just finished the main course and were looking at a dessert menu. Alyce had enjoyed the sun's dance on the water for its entire descent. Now it splayed its colors across the edge of the horizon in the most brilliant reds and oranges Alyce had ever seen. The darker clouds of a threatening storm had begun their sneaky encroachment on the sun's territory, but for now, it was standing its ground. It appeared the sun would win until it had finished its stellar finale for the evening.

Dinner had been delightful. More banter about movies they loved, books they'd read, items on their bucket list. Lots to talk about by the middle-aged couple at table 27, window-side view. To the outsider, it would appear these two had been in love for a long time. They were so engrossed in each other's words that the wait staff had been remiss to interrupt between each course. Twice Ben had put his hand on Alyce's. Once as they prayed over their meal, and once when Alyce talked about the day her beloved father had passed.

Now, as the sun slipped into a sliver of gold, Ben looked across the table and realized he couldn't let someone so special get away without trying. For the first time in a long while he was ready. He wanted to know more about her, but didn't know how far to delve. Alyce wondered why someone as charming and handsome as Ben had no woman in his life. He had spoken lovingly of his own parents and their relationship. One of them needed to break through the barrier of personal relationships and Ben decided he must be the one.

"Alyce," he said as he laid the dessert menu on the table and settled back in his chair, "what about you?"

"I'd love the key lime pie, but could we possibly share?" Alyce replied, innocently mistaking that he wondered what she'd be choosing for dessert. The way she tilted her head and gave him a slight smile when she asked totally disarmed him.

"Sure!" he said. "Key lime is one of my favorites."

The server took their dessert order, then refilled their water glasses as Alyce rose from her seat. "Would you direct me to the ladies' room?" she asked the young woman attending them. Glancing at Ben she said, "I'll be right back. Don't eat all of the pie!"

Ben laughed as he watched her walking away. She was lovely and elegant. He saw a couple of men taking notice as she passed. Alyce was oblivious. It was natural for her to make eye contact with a ready smile for everyone she met. There was an innocence that seemed more true to Alyce than the woman turning heads as she made her way between the tables. She was a keeper, and Ben could not fathom why anyone may have tossed her aside.

All Alyce thought as she made her way to the ladies' room was whether Ben was watching her walk away. One of her biggest fears was going out in public without remembering to check herself in the mirror from all angles. She hoped she'd done a thorough job.

She could tell he was ready to go deeper in their conversation and she simply was not sure what she was going to say about her husband. Or ex-husband. Or was he estranged? It was all too complicated.

When he'd placed his hand on hers, she was more aware than ever that she had no rings on her left hand. She'd removed them before the trip and left them in her jewelry box at home. It was a bold personal step to do so.

"Don't forget," she said to herself in the bathroom mirror, "it wasn't *your* choice to end up in this position."

Alyce washed her hands and made her way back to the table. Sitting down, she decided to be the aggressor and dive right in.

"My husband and I—well, I guess he's my husband—have been married for twenty-six years." Alyce swallowed, picked up her water glass and drank half of its contents, then set it down and began again.

"Over a year ago I discovered that for several months he had been in a relationship with a young associate at his office. I offered forgiveness and figured we would work through things. He declined, said he was already over the marriage, and moved out." She folded and unfolded the hem of her napkin as she spoke.

"Since then, I have been numb. Wandering around doing absolutely nothing to deal with this entire mess. I guess biding my time? Unsure of who I was and what I needed to do, or even wanted to do. Existing in a very broken state. I'm damaged goods," she said and looked Ben straight in the eye. As she did so, tears formed that threatened to spill when she blinked.

"You have made me feel valuable the past few days," Alyce said as two tiny rivulets made their way to the corners of her slight smile. She gently dabbed at them with her napkin. "And for that I truly cannot thank you enough. For not only listening to my lame stories, but for hearing me. I'm not going home the same as when I arrived. I have found something inside of me that I didn't know was missing. You did that for me, Ben. Thank you."

Ben was grateful that the key lime pie arrived at that very moment. Alyce's confession was a lot to process and he quickly did so, planning his next words very carefully in the span of about a minute.

He picked up his fork, cut off a small bite of pie, then set it back down on the plate without eating. His face was difficult to read. She wasn't sure what response she expected from him, but wasn't prepared for his next words.

"That was me," he said. He worked his jaw and pursed his lips as if trying to control a barrage of words from spilling onto the table. Ben wanted to speak carefully and began with deliberate control, "I did the same thing to my wife, only worse."

Ben realized that he was in jeopardy of spoiling their evening and, more importantly, their newfound friendship. What had he been thinking? Why would a woman intentionally walk into a relationship with a man with his track record? Why would she be the victim of infidelity, then choose friendship with another man who might do the same?

Knowing he had little or nothing to lose, he began to share. He had promised himself a long time ago that he would own his story if it meant another person or marriage could be saved. He'd imagined it helping someone about to step into adultery. He'd imagined his story helping someone avoid the trap of pornography or perhaps free themselves. He'd even imagined it helping a young man about to embark on the journey of marriage. But he'd never imagined helping a woman after her love had been abused by someone just like him. Wasn't it a little bizarre to think that she would even hear him out?

"Where is your husband now?" Ben asked quietly when he felt he had shared enough.

"Michael, that's his name, is in Nashville living in an apartment. He has a prestigious law practice with five partners, twelve junior associates, and an office overlooking the Cumberland River and the Titans stadium. He is very comfortable in all areas of his life as it relates to satisfying Michael. He has broken my trust and my heart, as well as the trust and hearts of our three children. He'll have no part of counseling or any attempt at saving our marriage. So, I must move on and be content to be single instead of enjoying this phase of my life with the man I love. Forgive me, Ben, but how could you do something like that to the person you'd promised to love forever?"

Alyce was calm. There were no longer tears, nor was there any anger in her voice. It was a bold and honest question to someone highly qualified to answer. But Ben was silent. He sat staring out at the water. Alyce, too, stared at the spot where she'd watched the sun quickly descend into a wink of light, then slide quietly and effortlessly over the edge of the world. Something poignant and stunning had disappeared with little notice, and for the first time ever, its performance left Alyce feeling empty and sad.

A server appeared at the table and filled their water glasses. Both felt weary, where minutes before they'd been alive and full of laughter and conversation.

"I won't make excuses," Ben answered, as the server walked away.

"I'm sorry?" Alyce asked, finally turning to look him in the eye.

"I will not make excuses for anyone regarding their selfish actions," Ben said. "I can only say that, even in the most impossible situations, God can always change a heart. No one deserves to be treated as you have been by Michael. My wife certainly did nothing to deserve what I did to her. Michael and I are guilty of something as old as time itself, being duped by the enemy of this world and convinced to trade our very souls for momentary thrills. To exchange eternal love for empty lusts. There is no excuse for that, only sorrow."

Ben had not realized that he had grown emotional. He looked into Alyce's eyes and felt the weight of his entire life fall fully onto his shoulders. He wondered if he'd ever completely lose the burden of his past. Perhaps not in its entirety.

Throughout dinner he had noticed lightning in the distance. Now it flashed closer on the horizon where once the red and gold swath of sunset had been. He swallowed hard, then said, "We've not talked about our faith so let me say to you that, while I carry deep regret as my companion, I have been given the gift of a Comforter who speaks to me and tells me every day that I have been redeemed. I don't know what you believe about God and Jesus, but I can tell you that I have been freed from my past and I know that the same can be true for you and your hurting heart." Ben hesitated before adding, "And, prayerfully, one day for Michael."

Alyce's eyes conveyed something Ben couldn't quite place. Her hurt was still a freshly opened wound and he expected her any minute to insist he take her back to the condo. Instead, Alyce reached out her hand to cover Ben's. She gave a slight smile, then spoke quietly.

"I know you've been deceived, Ben. I know it and it breaks my heart. I also have faith in my Redeemer. He can do miraculous things. My greatest struggle is that I believe, yet I felt God was simply choosing not to act on my behalf. Then, one day He graciously reminded me of two little words, *free will*." With that Alyce squeezed Ben's hand, picked up her fork, and took a bite of key lime pie.

She softly chewed and swallowed. Setting down the fork she decided to speak boldly. "Ben, life is full of choices, right?" He nodded in agreement. "I can't control another human being on this planet. God can, but He doesn't. Not because He doesn't love me, but because He does love me and wants me to be satisfied with Him over anyone or anything. He's not going to manipulate me or anyone *for* me. It has to be my free will choosing Him—every day and in every way—regardless of the particulars."

"He provides countless opportunities for us each to choose Him and His best. In the meantime, we become convinced that God is going to cheat us. That He doesn't quite understand or maybe He's missed the point about what would be mind-blowing chapters for our stories. So rather than let Him write, we take the pen from His hand and scribble away. Before long, the message of who we are is unclear to the world, and certainly unclear to ourselves."

"We grow angry and bitter, because we're convinced God has disappointed our hearts. We blame Him that our story is full of drama, rather than the beautiful love story we had imagined. I'm speaking for myself. I can't change Michael's life for him. I can only change the way I react by letting the Holy Spirit control me. And I can only relinquish my life as my heart is satisfied and I trust in His deep, abiding love for little old, sinful me."

Alyce's blue eyes sparkled as she spoke those last words. Ben felt the presence of God in their conversation. Wasn't that what he had prayed for before he left? He smiled and together they sat silently as the storm passed out at sea in a lightning display of grand magnitude. Ben picked up his fork. After they'd eaten over half the pie, he spoke.

"Taste and see that the LORD is good."

"Yes," Alyce agreed as a tremendous bolt of lightning struck far out in the water and, shortly after, thunder rumbled toward them, creating vibrations in the glass. She smiled again at Ben and, although neither knew what to say, they both seemed okay with that.

When the last of the pie was eaten and the waitress brought the check to the table, Ben finally spoke. As he tucked his credit card into the slot and placed it on the table he asked, "So, what shall we do now?"

The heaviest clouds appeared to be moving far down the beach. The darker daylight that lingers between sunset and nightfall had reappeared, and Alyce said, "It appears we have survived the worst of the storm. I think it's safe to head back."

Ben added a tip and signed his name to the receipt, tucking the pen inside the leather folder. "Yes, it does appear we've weathered this storm together," he said.

They smiled as they made their way from the restaurant. There was a comfort between them. Ben felt lighter in his spirit, even though he'd not imagined that was possible. Uncertain as to what this evening meant for their relationship, Alyce knew that God had given her the courage to say the things she'd said. Perhaps her entire trip had been for this specific moment.

As they drove back along the coast, Ben spoke up. "You know, this week has been like a spiritual retreat for me."

Alyce reacted, "I was just thinking the same thing."

"As a teenager, I never liked to go home after a retreat. You just knew there would be this incredible letdown."

"I know," Alyce said as she reached out and took Ben's hand. "But I always loved the new forever-friends I made."

As they turned into the condo, Alyce asked Ben if he wanted to change and meet on the beach to watch the stars come out. She didn't want their conversation to end. They walked to their separate elevators with an agreement to meet by the pool in fifteen minutes.

Alyce thought about their conversation and marveled at how clear her mind seemed and how free her spirit felt as the elevator lifted its way to her floor. The doors parted and there on the balcony stood a familiar figure.

"Hello, Alyce," he said.

Alyce swallowed hard and took a deep breath.

"Hello, Michael," she said.

Chapter Thirteen

MICHAEL

*T*wo days before, Michael had begun digging around in their credit card records, trying to figure out where in the world Alyce had gone. The irony was not lost on him that this was how Alyce had discovered his infidelity. Back then, he had the buffer of knowing she wasn't paying much attention to the bills when they came. In truth, she had rarely even given them a thought, always trusting him to handle their business and accounting.

It was chance—or was it—that she had happened to check the bill back in July. Alyce ordered Michael a handsome, leather portfolio as a surprise, then realized the charge could show on their bill before it arrived and she'd given it to him. She'd pulled up their statement to keep an eye out for it.

Of course it would be the same month that he'd treated Cassidy to a massage on two separate occasions. He hated massages so he couldn't claim them as for himself. When Alyce confronted him, he did manage to pass it off as a client expense. But that piqued her suspicions. She soon uncovered other evidence of his indiscretions.

He had underestimated Alyce. There was no trace of her current whereabouts on the credit card bill. Michael had to admit he was stumped. He didn't dare ask the kids where their mother had gone. He wanted no one to know he was looking for her. There was his pride to think about, even though he had but one mission—to find Alyce and beg her to forgive him.

He needed to know if their marriage could be saved. But just in case she totally shunned him, he didn't want anyone to know he'd tried. Michael wasn't quite humbled enough to be looking for personal restoration. He merely wanted his old life back and couldn't quite grasp that Alyce wasn't ardently waiting for him at home.

He hated to admit it, but he had resorted to breaking and entering—again—in order to find clues. He'd thought about using Cassidy's Facebook page to look for leads. He didn't engage in social media, but he'd do anything to uncover Alyce's location. However, he couldn't search Facebook because he'd already told Cassidy they were finished. She'd wasted no time getting her things from his apartment and moving on.

Michael hoped she would also quit her job when he told her they were done, but so far Cassidy acted as if nothing had ever happened between them. He had solicited Carrie's help in a feigned interest to learn more about Instagram. Together they had looked up various members of the firm, including Cassidy, where they discovered pictures that violated firm social media policies. If she didn't choose to go, he would have one of the partners fire her for these obvious reasons.

But for now, his woes with Cassidy were small potatoes in relation to his quest to find his wife. What had he been thinking? He knew the answer to that question. He wasn't thinking at all. Or maybe he should admit he'd only been thinking of himself for some time now. It was as if a fog was beginning to clear from his mind and his thoughts were more lucid than they had been in years. He had to find her, but thus far everything had been a dead end.

So, he'd gone back to their home under cover of night. Was it fair for him to call it theirs anymore? He had his doubts. This time he had been careful to avoid triggering the alarm system. It still amazed him how differently the house looked inside, even though she hadn't begun to complete all her projects. Michael felt hopeful at the prospect of the two of them finishing it together.

The first thing he did once back inside the house was look for their divorce papers. He prayed she'd not signed them as he had, but even if so, nothing was finalized unless a judge decreed. They could be shredded and burned in his opinion. If he found them unsigned, he would view that as a positive.

Michael was beginning to realize that he was partly to blame for the staleness of their marriage. He had wanted her to be more fun and expressed to her his boredom. Why couldn't he see that she was limited by his unwillingness to allow her to evolve and grow? Truth be told, he wanted the familiarity of her predictability while he ventured out and played. He wanted her to remain stuck in her role as defined by motherhood and her identity as his wife, while he experimented and tested the waters that provided a thrill and opened new doors.

Like a kid, he wanted to always have his favorite vanilla ice cream while sampling some crazy flavors. Never once did it occur to him that she might long to do the same, not with other people, but within their life together. They could have been doing this together all along.

Selfishness was a quality he loathed. He could feel the hypocrisy of the giant log in his eye.

Searching through the items on the dining room table, Michael was careful not to disrupt the piles Alyce had painstakingly created. He thought perhaps he'd find a brochure with clues to her whereabouts or a phone number written on a piece of paper. But there had been nothing on the table or in the kitchen or the bedroom. How was he going to find where Alyce had gone?

He was so desperate to find a clue that he even searched through the trash cans. It was getting late. Weary, he plopped down onto the sofa in the family room. Looking around at the pictures on the wall and lining the bookcases, Michael felt ashamed of himself for the first time. How badly he knew he had hurt Alyce, his best friend in the entire world. Like a kid on Christmas morning, Michael had been given what he had always asked for in the family and life they had created. But when something shiny caught his eye, he'd laid them aside, assuming they'd always be there when the shiny lost its luster.

The faces of his children looked at him from the shelves, as did a photo of his mom and dad from their fiftieth wedding anniversary celebration. What an example of love they had effortlessly provided. They had been gone for three years now, victims of a drunk driver who plowed through a red light. His mother would have been devastated by his behavior. He felt relief that his father never knew him as this man he had become.

Michael began to weep. His shoulders heaved and the sound of his wailing carried throughout the empty house. This wasn't who he was. He couldn't even remember how he'd started down this road of lies and infidelity and callousness toward his wife and family. "Alyce, where are you?" he cried out into the nothingness.

His eyes fell upon Alyce's stack of books beside her chair. He stood and walked over to search them. Maybe she'd written something in a journal or stuck information inside a book. The chair held the familiar embrace of her scent and as the arms of the chair welcomed him in consolation, he wept long and hard and bitterly, until, utterly exhausted, he'd fallen asleep.

Michael wasn't sure how long he slept in Alyce's chair, but when he woke it was first light. The sun was not yet visible, but the familiar blackness of the trees silhouetted against the porpoise-gray sky of early dawn was a welcome sight. He'd forgotten how beautiful every moment was in their little corner of life.

He sat up and wiped his hand across his face, yawning widely. Walking into the kitchen, he was relieved to see that all the coffee fixings were exactly where they'd always been. Alyce had added a new coffee pot that freshly ground the beans, placing it beside their single serving brewer. He never knew she wanted one of those.

He would have loved to try it out now, but knew he was inclined to break it. He pulled his favorite mug from the cabinet and popped a K-cup in the Keurig. Steaming cup in hand, Michael returned to the sanctuary of Alyce's chair.

How he'd despised her sitting in that chair when the truth was revealed about his affair. She'd been angry and hurt and harsh words had been exchanged, but nothing fanned his anger like seeing her sitting there, reading her Bible, with tears streaming down her face. He knew she was praying for him, for them, and it infuriated him. The rub of deeply ingrained truths against his rising demand for self-gratification caused him to chafe. If she'd been a better wife, he'd convinced himself, he wouldn't have been forced to go elsewhere.

Now, he picked up one of several translations of the Bible she kept and opened it, skimming the various notes she'd written in the margin. Michael read the spine of each of the books beside the chair, surprised to find a book of poetry mingled with the titles of secular and religious books stacked there. On the end table where her lamp was always lit, he saw her familiar stash of highlighters, Post-It notes, and pens. Organized chaos was what she liked to call it.

He took a deep drink of the hot liquid, helping to clear the cobwebs. His eyes were slightly swollen from crying so hard the night before. Michael thought he'd go to the half bath and splash some cold water on his face, but as he stood a single piece of paper caught his eye. There on the floor, where he felt certain he should have noticed it, was a bright pink Post-It with the words *Pelican Pointe* and a phone number. Could this be his lead to Alyce? Michael was elated.

He did a quick Google search of the area code to determine the city, then he looked up Pelican Pointe. It appeared Alyce was in Orange Beach, Alabama. He was convinced it was so. How in the world had she ended up there? He felt she would be home in a day or so, but he could not wait any longer. Besides, if she was going to reject him, wouldn't it be easier to be far away from home when it happened?

He called Carrie and asked her to clear his schedule for the next three days and to please arrange the earliest possible flight to Pensacola. He would need a rental car. Only a one-way ticket, as he was uncertain as to when and how he would return. Maybe he could make the drive back home with Alyce.

Everything was falling into place. Michael was full of hope that finding the piece of paper was a miracle. He would pray all the way to her that she would hear his heart and take him back. Surely God would be on his side. Hadn't he provided the clue for which Michael was searching?

Adrenaline pumping, Michael's next step was heading to his apartment to pack a bag. As he opened the back door to leave their home, the dent in his Maserati reminded him to set the alarm. He didn't know what awaited him, but he knew he could not wait for her to return. Every day apart could widen the gap between them. A gap he had single-handedly created.

When Michael arrived at Pelican Pointe, he was surprised at how nice it was. Where had Alyce gotten the money to stay here without using her credit card? After flashing his identification and regaling the desk clerk with a fake story about surprising his wife for her birthday, Michael was unable to secure a key, but he did get her room number.

He was a nervous wreck as he stepped from the elevator into the hallway outside her door. It took a tremendous amount of courage, but he finally gathered himself and knocked. He rang the doorbell. No sounds came from within. Two more attempts garnered no response. He knew she was here somewhere, because he'd seen her car in the garage.

Michael made a trip to the pool area and scanned the beach, but a sudden storm forced him back inside. He decided to wait in the lobby, passing the time by imagining a variety of scenarios for Alyce's reaction when she saw him there. A half hour ticked by and he decided to try her room again. Maybe he'd missed her coming in while out on the beach.

Michael had knocked loudly and rung the bell when he heard the elevator making its way from below. Something told him that Alyce would step through the doors when it arrived. He said a quick prayer as he positioned himself to greet her. Leaning against the rail, he tried to appear casual by crossing his arms on his chest and his feet at the ankles. He was not prepared for the beautiful, vibrant woman who emerged through the open elevator doors. She quite honestly took his breath away. Alyce had been out. But with whom? She looked at him, startled at his presence. He said the only thing he knew to say.

"Hello, Alyce."

Chapter Fourteen
MICHAEL / ALYCE / BEN

*A*lyce watched her husband as he sat in the chair by the window, staring out at the darkness. It had not fully registered that he was actually in Orange Beach and in her condo. She moved about in the kitchen making a pot of coffee and avoiding the inevitable. He was going to question everything and she knew it.

Honestly, how dare he? She owed him no explanations. Not the first one. Alyce's brain could not formulate thoughts to build words into rational phrases, so the two remained in silence. Michael was reeling from the blows of reality that so skewed his preconceived expectations. It was messing with his mind. He had imagined many scenarios at his arrival. None of them remotely resembled the one playing out before him now.

When Michael turned to look her way, Alyce shifted her full focus to making the coffee. She felt his gaze on her every move and didn't like the way she felt. Disgust. Normally she would have been thrilled at the way his eyes followed her, but now? Anger. These were the best adjectives she could find, though they hardly scratched the surface of her emotions. Like describing a brutal massacre with the single word *murder*, Alyce felt inadequate to mentally verbalize the carnage of her soul, much less give voice to it.

She felt she'd already messed up by inviting him in, but what could she do? She excused herself to change clothes. Closing the bedroom door behind her, she sat on the end of the bed to think. The problem was she didn't know *what* to think.

What do you know? Alyce asked herself.

But, try as she might, the only thing she *knew* was that her husband was in the next room acting as if this surprise visit was planned between the two of them. And somehow she felt she had been caught in the wrong. But nothing could have been further from the truth.

When she had initially emerged from the elevator she wanted to freak out. However, she had drawn a deep breath and brilliantly maintained a quiet composure. *Holy Spirit in, Alyce out.*

Alyce stood to her feet and carefully removed her dress. She hung it precisely on the hanger, taking time to cover it with the plastic bag for protection, before picking up her gym shorts and T-shirt where she'd dropped them on the bed only a few hours before.

It dawned on her how much she had relaxed this past week. She felt truer to herself than she had since graduating college. More in control. Now, she took her time before going out to face Michael. This thing between them had escalated to all-out war. In coming to the beach, she had retreated to neutral territory to regroup and heal. He had brought the battlefront to her. She could decide whether it was worth the energy to fight.

Sitting on the edge of the bed to gather her thoughts, the words she'd written on an index card stared back at her from the nightstand. It was a quote from Oswald Chambers.

"When we do something out of a sense of duty, it is easy to explain the reasons for our actions to others. But when we do something out of obedience to the LORD, there can be no other explanation—just obedience."

How long had she embraced the message of this encouragement? It had been a long time since she'd felt love for her husband. For months she had loved him out of obedience to the LORD, because she loved *Him*, which required no explanation. She assumed that many thought the motivation for her faithfulness was obligation to Michael or fear of being alone without his support. But the quote had served as a necessary, daily reminder, lest she despair because she felt so unloved. On the opposite side of the same card she had written these paraphrased words of Martin Luther:

> *"Feelings come and feelings go*
> *And feelings are deceiving*
> *But hope is in the word of God*
> *None else is worth believing."*

Every nugget of the beautiful conversation she had just shared with Ben over dessert was resting gently on Alyce's psyche. She felt a blessed calm in her very core that assured her that God was in control of the situation. Remembering the conversation reminded her of Ben. He would be waiting beside the pool. She should text him and excuse herself. Would he accept that without pushing for further explanation?

Alyce knew that this entire situation demanded prayer. She dropped to her knees and fell silent before the LORD. Somehow she sensed that

He was allowing her to witness the beginning of new chapters not only for herself, but also for Michael and for Ben.

"I don't know what's going on, Father, but I am totally at peace with whatever comes. You've been so faithful to me, especially in my freak-out moments when I let my eyes lock on my circumstances rather than my Deliverer. Not that You need me to say this, but Your track record speaks for itself and I am so totally okay with letting You continue to lead. I wish I could stay right here in this very spot and not emerge until everything is sorted out, but I recognize my role in what is to come. So, I lay it all down and rest in You. Fill me and move and breathe as me. I surrender to You, my God and my King. You are Faithful and True."

Alyce was suddenly aware that Michael was talking with someone. She hopped up from the floor and rushed from the room to find Michael asking, "I'm sorry. Who are you?" to Ben's startled face at her door. Snatching up flip-flops, she headed for the two standing in the doorway.

In one fluid motion she said, "Michael, make yourself a cup of coffee and I will be back," brushing past him and grabbing Ben's hand along the way. She prayed that the elevator was still on her floor and the doors would open...NOW!

They did! Alyce pulled Ben along into the elevator and held up a finger as a signal to Michael to wait, as he continued to stand, stunned, in the door of her condo. The elevator doors shut and Alyce leaned back on the wall and closed her eyes. *Alyce out, Holy Spirit in. Alyce out, Holy Spirit in.*

Opening her eyes, she realized that she hadn't pressed a button. She reached out and pressed the "G" for ground and looked up at Ben with a sheepish smile.

"That was Michael."

"So I presumed." Ben seemed amused.

"I had no idea."

"Obviously."

They looked at each other for a moment, then Alyce burst out a laugh. She pressed her fingers to her lips, but it was no use. The giggles overtook her. Ben began to chuckle. Their laughter gained momentum as the elevator descended. When the doors opened, Alyce made a beeline toward the ladies' restroom.

"I can't even!" she shrieked as she backed her way into the cool, tile sanctuary away from the madness. Thankfully, no one else was present at this time of night. They would surely have assumed she was drunk.

Was this it? Was she finally losing it? Had Michael's antics driven her into stark-raving lunacy? She looked at herself in the warm bathroom light. A big, goofy grin spread across her face. Everything about her looked the same as one hour before. Her makeup was pristine. Her hair looked ridiculously good, despite pulling the T-shirt over her head.

Suddenly horrified, Alyce realized that in blindly changing into her other clothes, she had grabbed a T-shirt Harrison had given her as a joke. She only wore it around him to be funny, but it was super comfortable so she'd brought it with her to wear while hanging out in the condo. Now, staring back at her, she burst into laughter again. "I'M TOO SEXY FOR THIS SHIRT," was emblazoned across her front.

Gathering her composure and awkwardly hugging herself to hide the word sexy, Alyce emerged to find no trace of Ben. He wasn't in the lobby. She waited politely, assuming he, too, had to use the facilities. After several minutes passed, she walked to the wall of windows that overlooked the pool and stood staring past it at the beautiful ocean beyond. The moon had come out fully now and frosted the surface of the water with a thin layer of light.

What had happened to her beautiful evening? She should be lying on the beach on a blanket looking up at the stars and sharing more of herself with this charming, God-loving man she'd just met. No assumptions. No inappropriate banter. Just fabulous conversation with a man who held no agenda of his own but to be her friend.

"We can still go out there," a voice said behind her. Ben had quietly walked up and seemed to read her mind. "I had already set us up on the beach. Nice shirt, by the way."

"Let's go!" Alyce said as she pushed open the glass door and ran along the path beyond the pool and down the steps to the beach.

She did not feel one ounce of guilt for leaving Michael alone and waiting in her room. Together they walked to where Ben had spread two blankets on the sand. *Always the gentleman*, Alyce thought.

They reclined and lay there in a comfortable silence, staring up at the velvety sky. She had nothing to say, but Ben seemed to expect nothing from her. She found herself reaching out through the darkness for his hand. That was all. Just a hand to hold while she processed.

It startled her when she realized that tears were rolling from the corners of her eyes and making their way into her hairline. She used the back of her hand to brush them away, but they continued to come so frequently that she could not keep up.

Ben broke the silence, "There's an old hymn that says, *Jesus I am resting, resting, in the joy of what Thou art. I am finding out the greatness of Thy loving heart. Thou hast bid me gaze upon Thee and Thy beauty fills my soul, for by Thy transforming power, Thou hast made me whole.*

"In Hebrews 4—that's a passage I've been studying—we're encouraged to rest in the sufficiency of Christ—sort of like you were saying at dinner. Did you know that we don't even know the author of Hebrews? What a great book! I love that God chose to use an unknown to write us an entire book about His sufficiency. That means I can't say, 'Sure, but that guy never had to go through what I've been through,' because I don't know who he was and have no idea what his life was like. Maybe he could have written my exact story as his own. His message was simply to remind us that no matter what, God was satisfied by the fullness of creation. And so, on day seven, He rested. It was enough. Sufficient. He wants us to be satisfied with His work on our behalf. To rest in His sufficiency as He sees us complete in Him."

"Be still," Alyce spoke, "and I will fight for you. Exodus 14:14."

"Precisely," Ben agreed. "He loves us all, Alyce. You, me, and that misguided soul upstairs in your condo. And His promise to us, as a man of His word, is that He is able and He is willing, to make sufficient provision for us. We simply can't do any of this on our own. And most often, we aren't really willing to do what would be necessary. His provision is perfect and His supply is overflowing."

Alyce said, "I have come to these same realizations this past year, but what does all this mean now? I thought it meant I wouldn't have to worry once I was single. I thought it meant He was going to take care of me no matter what, *after* the divorce. I'm scared, Ben. I don't really have any desire to go up there and entertain conversation with him. I don't trust him. I don't even feel love for him at this moment. Can I love or trust him again?"

Ben sat upright on his blanket and spoke as he gazed out at the moonlit ocean.

"When my wife and I were in counseling, a wise man told us that Amie would never trust me again. I didn't like those odds. Then he said in truth she never should have. We were shocked. He looked at me and said I couldn't trust her either. You can imagine Amie's face when he said that!" Ben paused as if he were seeing it again. "That man said the only thing trustworthy in any human being is what we see Christ doing in each other. I mean, think about it. Isn't that so? You and I, right here and now, feel a connection of trust because we are sharing from our hearts what Christ has done in our lives. That is the best feeling ever. When a couple shares that in a marriage, I can only imagine what freedom they find to love each other. They're each loving *from* the Jesus in them, and they're *in love with* the Jesus in their partner. I can't imagine any hurt that can't be overcome in a scenario like that."

"I agree, but right this moment I have a bunker of protection around my heart. I thought Michael *did* love Jesus. We were in church from the time we began dating, and he taught a small group for eighteen years. He even went to an early-morning men's group once a week. There is no pain or shame like that of being duped by someone you love. I don't ever want to hurt like that again. I don't think I can."

Ben waited a moment as he processed and prayed for God to guard and guide his words. "Tim Keller said, 'The longer the love, the deeper the love, the greater the torment of its loss.' I believe the anxiety you feel at the thought of surrendering your heart again to Michael is fueled by the torment you have felt over the loss of something so deep and enduring being stripped from you. But, hey, you haven't even given Michael a chance to speak. Do you know why he's here?"

Alyce sat up and faced Ben. The ridiculousness of that reality hit her squarely in the gut. She had no idea why Michael had come. What if he'd come to stand over her as she signed the divorce papers? She honestly couldn't say. Like an awkward middle schooler, she had darted out and left him standing with his mouth open.

She stood to her feet and Ben followed suit. She looked back up at the condos and the light shining from her unit. What waited for her when she returned? Further rejection? Remorse? Who was that man up there? Could she ever trust anything from his mouth again?

Ben spoke. "Alyce, when we say our vows, we promise 'for better or for worse.' And we mean it at the time. If there were sickness you'd stand by your word. If there were poverty you'd surely stand right by his side. If it helps to imagine his 'worse' as a sickness and poverty of the soul, then so be it. I have quickly surmised that you are not one who gives up. But we all need a pep talk sometimes. Maybe God knew you'd be the one to love Michael through all of this. I think you'd never forgive yourself if you didn't at least go see what he's got to say."

Alyce took a deep breath in. "I know that wherever I go, God goes before me. A cloud by day and a pillar of fire by night."

"That's a good word," Ben said. "Before you go up, could I pray with you?"

Alyce stepped closer to Ben and bowed her head as he placed his hands on her shoulders. "LORD, we are grateful. We're somewhat confused right now, but we thank You that You're not. There's not a thing in either of us that is confident as we look on the circumstance, but when we fix our eyes on You, Father, we can see nothing but Your sweet peace and gentle love that washes over us and fills us with strength for today and hope for tomorrow. We thank You that You haven't given us a spirit of fear, but a spirit of power and love and a sound mind. We ask that You overwhelm Alyce with that Spirit for whatever transpires in her talks with Michael. Forgive us the doubts and insecurities that cause us to sink when we take our eyes off You. We cling to the promise that You never leave us or forsake us. And, LORD, we do love You with all our hearts. Amen."

Ben and Alyce stood with their heads bowed together, and Ben was surprised when Alyce softly began singing,

Simply trusting Thee, Lord Jesus, I behold Thee as Thou art,
And Thy love so pure, so changeless,
Satisfies my heart;
Satisfies its deepest longings,
Meets, supplies its every need,
Compasseth me round with blessings;
Thine is love indeed.
Jesus I am resting, resting,
In the joy of what Thou art.
I am finding out the greatness of Thy loving heart.

They looked in each other's eyes and Alyce said, "You're not the only one who knows that song, but thank you for reminding me."

She hugged Ben tightly and silently breathed a prayer for God to give them both strength to face whatever came their way. Then she turned and began the walk to the stairs that led inside. To what, she did not even care.

Chapter Fifteen

MICHAEL / ALYCE

*A*lyce quietly let herself in. She didn't want to wake Michael if he might be sleeping. Michael would have laughed at the very idea of sleep. He hadn't slept more than a couple of hours since he'd booked his flight, and at that very moment, every nerve in his body was on high alert. He didn't recall ever feeling so out of control and at the mercy of another individual. It shocked him to realize these feelings of anxiety for Alyce's return.

Life for Michael had gone fairly as planned since he was a boy. He saw something he wanted. He worked hard and went after it. It became his. Some things he acquired didn't hold their value for him. In truth, very little did, a byproduct of ingratitude. But now he wasn't sure what was going on. He was actually nervous that Alyce wouldn't even engage in conversation after he'd come all this way.

It had proven a good thing that Alyce left with that guy—what did he say his name was? Ben? Michael had much to process regarding all he had encountered since his arrival. He was full of questions and wondering if he'd ever get any answers when she walked through the door. This Alyce was not someone he knew.

He noticed when she left that she was wearing the T-shirt Harrison had given her as a joke. Did she intend to do that? He couldn't imagine so, but then he didn't expect to find his wife looking so smoking hot when she stepped from the elevator. That white dress was not like anything he'd ever seen her wear. And since when did she tan? Her hair seemed lighter and she'd changed the cut. He was confused by it all.

He had planned this out in his mind the entire flight. He would find her sitting alone, watching reruns of Andy Griffith and eating pretzels and peanut butter to save money. She would be shocked to see him, but she would rush into his open arms when he told her he was sorry and had come to carry her home.

She would be relieved. He couldn't imagine what she'd done the past few days alone at the beach. Well, he now knew what she'd apparently been up to. Definitely not pining for him. What had gotten into her?

He stood nervously when she opened the door. He didn't know what to do with himself.

Alyce crossed over to her chair, stopping to slide open the glass door before sitting. Tucking her bare feet under her, she sat and motioned for him to do likewise.

"I see you got some coffee," she said. "Did you eat any dinner?"

He opened his mouth to answer, but before he could she continued, "I had some lovely sushi downstairs the other night with crème brûlée for dessert. You can have something sent up. Or there's fruit in the fridge."

Typically, at least in the "old days," Alyce would not have sat down until she'd made sure he had something to eat. She would have fussed over him and made him feel like a king. He was devastated. Michael responded, but his voice broke awkwardly when he said, "I think I'm fine, thanks. I haven't had much of an appetite today."

"So…" Alyce said, letting it hang in the air between them. She looked directly at Michael for a response.

"So," Michael began, "How in the world did you end up here?"

Alyce looked at him quizzically. At first, she thought what a ridiculous question to ask after nine months of separation and over a yearlong affair. But then she guessed that was as good a place as any to break the ice.

"My new friend, Salli, has been coming down here for several years now. She recommended this place to me a couple of months back when I mentioned getting away. It's been fantastic."

Michael relaxed a bit. "Oh! So, this is her place," he quickly said, assuming he was beginning to solve the mystery of how Alyce booked it and paid for it without his assistance.

"No," Alyce said nonchalantly. "They just like staying here." She was careful not to reveal too much. He was on her territory now and she was not releasing the upper hand for anything. What was it he liked to quote from the courtroom? Asked and answered? That was how this was going to transpire. He'd ask a question and she'd give a succinct answer.

She was full of questions herself, but didn't care to let him know anything mattered. She was calm, cool, and collected. Alyce stretched out her tan leg, working her knee that sometimes grew stiff.

"Still having trouble with that knee?" Michael asked. He winced. What was this line of cursory questioning? Excruciating, that's what it was. Here he sat with a woman with whom he'd shared a bed for over twenty-six years, yet they were complete strangers.

"A bit," Alyce acquiesced, "but I'm doing Tai Chi and it seems to be helping."

Tai Chi? Michael was totally confused. What in the world was going on with his wife? He sat up a little straighter and asked, "Who is Salli?"

Alyce stuck to her plan. "My new friend."

"And…how do you know her?"

"We met at my writing class."

"You're writing now?"

"I've always written. Mostly poetry. I joined a writer's guild to sharpen my skills."

Michael felt like a reporter in a bad interview. He was asking all the questions and getting simple, direct answers. Alyce typically gave him too much when responding, something he desperately wanted right about now. Didn't she wonder why he was there? Where was the woman who wept in her chair over him and over their marriage? She didn't seem callous, just genuinely disinterested.

Alyce wondered how to interact with Michael. Should she be direct and ask what he was doing there? She didn't want to shut him down, but she didn't feel led to help him in any way. For months she had lived at his every whim, hopeful that he would wake up and come to his senses. That he would at least meet her halfway and go to counseling.

She would concede that every marriage had issues. Human beings were ever evolving and change was inevitable, but also necessary. Honestly, she was grateful for many of the things that had transpired for her since discovering Michael's affair. She had no idea how bored she was with the routine. And she would never have imagined the person she was today lived inside her.

This brief time apart from life at home meant one thing for certain; she was returning a new and better version of herself. Alyce purposed in her heart that every morning she was going to ask God what great adventure He had planned for her that day. She was bolder. There was a new awareness of her value beyond the critical years of raising a family. Alyce had been created for that role, but it was a temporary position. Now her goal was to fulfill her next purpose. Life was far from over.

For years she'd lived through her children's accomplishments. Michael had provided for their family and she trusted him with decisions regarding their lives. But she had to wonder if, while being carefree, she'd lost some of her ability to care for herself.

They had been busy with good things. Somewhere along the way they'd forgotten to stay connected to one another. They knew Maggie, Lillian, and Harrison would leave home, but somehow expected life to default to a sort of pre-children norm. However, those original two people were no longer viable. Alyce and Michael were changed, yet, like many couples, assumed it would all magically be okay.

Alyce was distracted in her role as mom. There was homework and dance lessons and orthodontists and art classes and baseball tournaments. Mingled with the responsibilities of caring for their home, Alyce's calling became all-consuming. It came with no job description. You learned as you went and it was tough. It was a position she loved, but, done well, worked itself out of a job. Just as you felt you'd mastered it, the kids moved on. It seemed Alyce had become her own missing person.

As the kids became independent, Alyce did ask for money to do projects around the house, but by that time Michael was working so much that he used their home more like a dormitory than a haven, which is what she longed to create for the two of them. They'd had so many plans for the house. Fabulous dreams for when they were older and freer.

In the past, all these thoughts would have sent her into a fit of tears. But that was the old Alyce. The new Alyce was surrendered to the Spirit more than she ever dreamed possible. She was not merely resigned to her lot in life. She was free and open to whatever new thing her Father had planned, because she knew it would be so very good.

"Alyce?" Michael was saying. She didn't realize she had gotten inside her own head. She looked up as he said, "I was asking how are you?"

She sat upright in the chair, crossing her legs.

"You know, I'm better than I've ever been."

"Well, I must admit, you look fantastic. A fellow could get a complex if he wasn't careful."

Alyce smiled to herself and murmured a thank you. She really looked at Michael for the first time in a while. He was grayer and his features seemed sharper. His lean physique was still intact. Michael had always been a handsome man, a little dark and mysterious.

He'd often joke that she was the lighter side of him, his little sprite or fairy. Michael's demeanor could be ominous and what made him one of the most sought-after defense attorneys in Tennessee. He would often come in from work and seek her perspective on an issue, because he was not gifted with mercy. They balanced each other, but also brought out hidden qualities, such as Michael's dry wit. He could be hilarious when he relaxed.

Watching her typically strong, confident husband struggling to connect made Alyce want to relent, but she knew it was not the time for that.

Thank You, LORD, for fighting for me. I want to be still.

"What brings you to Orange Beach, Michael? Business?"

Maybe it was the way she asked, but Michael couldn't bear the formality between them. He slumped forward with his head down, elbows on his knees. "I've screwed up, Alyce. I've dug a deep hole for myself and I'm not sure I can climb out." He looked up at her without shifting his posture. "I've treated you horribly. I've nearly lost my family. I thought I was finally living, but it turns out I was ruining my life."

Alyce didn't flinch. It seemed she was an observer in this unfolding drama, not a participant. Watching for something…what was it? Maybe a bit of Jesus in Michael that she could trust? Was it even kind to expect that from him at this point?

"What happened, Michael?" He looked at her, somewhat unsure of what she meant. "I mean, last week you were texting me to find out when I'd return signed divorce papers. Did you have an epiphany?" Suddenly a thought popped into her head, "Oh, Cassidy left you; is that it?"

To her surprise, Michael didn't explode as anticipated. He put his face in his hands and wept. She wanted to go to his side and console him, but thankfully there was something keeping her calmly fixed to her spot.

Unmoved it seemed, she patiently waited while he regained enough composure to speak. As he did, he wiped tears and broke down again and again.

"I honestly don't know. I don't recognize who I've become. I've been self-seeking and living for the next gratification."

Alyce found it difficult not to respond with a rousing, *"Amen!"*

"You don't deserve this kind of treatment. You've always been a genuinely good person and you're an incredible mom. Why did I ever think some twenty-eight-year-old..."

Alyce gasped, "That's almost Maggie's age!"

"I know!" Michael wailed.

"Michael, you have got to get yourself together. I've never seen you like this and I'm not sure we are accomplishing a thing."

Alyce walked to the kitchen to get him some water. When she came back and handed him the glass he grabbed her hand. Instinctively, Alyce pulled it away and went back to her chair. She tossed a box of tissues onto the couch beside him.

"Alyce, I am so very sorry," Michael said. "From the depths of my heart I want you to know that."

"I believe you, Michael. I'm just not sure what it means to me at this point."

They sat in silence for several minutes, neither one looking at the other. When Michael spoke, it was more clearly and evenly.

"I will spend the rest of my life showing you how sorry I am."

Alyce waited to respond, then said, "I don't know what our future looks like anymore. I'm really tired. It has been a long day. I will get you a pillow and a blanket. I asked downstairs if they had another room for you, but they don't. You may sleep on the couch tonight and we can talk more in the morning. You can use the bathroom before I go in and lock the door."

She walked into her room and emerged with a blanket over one arm and a pillow under the other. Alyce felt calm and resolute. She sat down on the edge of the coffee table in front of Michael. They were face-to-face for the first time in months. She was sad and weary and briefly wished they could crawl into bed together and spoon like they'd done so many times.

She wanted her Michael back, not this man who seemed emotionally unstable and unsure of himself. He looked deeply into her eyes, searching for a sign of hope. She gave him none. Just a look of pity.

"Michael," Alyce said. "You are still my husband for now. We have shared more together than we have apart. I would not even begin to try and sort this out tonight, but I will go to my room to pray and process. I suggest you do the same. In the morning, if I come out and you're still here and this hasn't been some freak-out moment on your part, we will have a rational conversation. For now, let's leave it alone and try to get some rest. Okay?"

Michael nodded. He was exhausted. Even though things hadn't been what he expected, it was a start. He got up and went into the bathroom. When he came out, Alyce was cleaning up the coffee and preparing the pot for the next morning. Some things never changed. But he loved that about her. He loved her.

Michael stretched out on the sofa. Alyce stopped to turn off the lamp by her chair.

"Good night, Alyce," Michael said.

"Good night."

Chapter Sixteen

ALYCE

*A*lyce had tossed and turned a fair amount before finally succumbing to emotional exhaustion and, thankfully, sleep. When she first woke, the shadowy room seemed like every other morning she'd awakened there.

Mindlessly staring at the room-darkening drapes, she applauded the genius who invented them. The dark room explained why she'd slept so late every morning since she'd arrived. Of course, eight o'clock was late for her. Perhaps she should consider adding these to her bedroom at home. That's when she remembered everything had changed.

She tried to arrange her waking thoughts. Alyce longed to keep the mental drapes drawn tightly against the harsh realities that awaited her this morning. She sat up, drew her knees to her chest, and hugged them tightly, her eyes fixed on the bedroom door.

She felt she was prayed out. God had heard her heart over and over before she slept. Now, she needed to be still and listen. He wanted to show her new things about His character and glory. She wanted desperately to hear them.

There was not a sound from the other side of the bedroom door. She continued to stare at it, wondering if Michael was still sleeping or if he'd slept at all.

"LORD, I'm listening," Alyce said softly into the sacred stillness.

Her spirit was willing, but her flesh was struggling. She glanced at the clock, shocked to see that it was almost 8:30. To sleep that late despite everything meant one of two things. Either her body and mind had withdrawn from the conflict and shut down, or she was truly at peace with the situation and it had freed her mind to rest, once she settled in.

Oddly, she felt the latter was true. Supernatural peace had eventually overwhelmed her and she knew that God was at work. She needed only to be still, which was proving to be an issue. Alyce was restless this morning. Maybe a walk on the beach was the better place to listen.

A sudden knock startled her.

"Alyce?" Michael's voice came meekly from the other side. "I'm sorry, babe, but I've really got to use the bathroom."

Alyce found that amusing. She suppressed a grin and replied, "It's unlocked. You can come through, but do not look at me!"

Michael darted to the bathroom and shut the door. Something familiar refreshed its memory in Alyce's mind. The juxtaposition of two normals was quirky and unsettling. As sounds of Michael washing his hands came from the other side of the door, Alyce plumped the pillows, leaned back against them, and straightened the covers around her. She brushed her fingers through her hair, thinking she shouldn't care, but caring nonetheless. She hoped she looked relaxed and serene. Every time he looked at her, she wanted him to see all that he was risking and all that she was becoming without him.

He emerged from the bathroom awkwardly. She could tell he was weighing whether he could engage her in conversation. Keeping his eyes averted, he asked if she slept.

"I did," Alyce said. Not particularly in the luxuriating way she wanted him to believe, but she did sleep. It was not necessary to let him know he was able to steal one moment of her life that she did not willingly surrender. Alyce needed to maintain control for as long as possible.

He ventured a glance her way.

"I said don't look at me!" Alyce quickly reminded him. She sounded like a thirteen-year-old rather than an adult. It dawned on her that this was exactly how she had felt for the past nine months; like a preteen girl playing games. Instead of a confident, self-respecting woman, the secrets and lies and he said/she said antics made her feel silly and immature. They were middle school romance distractions, which she had always abhorred and refused to engage.

Michael placed his hand beside his eye to block his view. Alyce used her advantage to check out her husband. He had slept in his boxers and darted through wearing nothing else. Michael was attractive to her. Tall and lean, not particularly muscular, but even with a bit of middle-age paunch, she appreciated his physique.

"Did you not bring a suitcase—meaning gym shorts—with you?"

"I never got it out of the rental last night."

"Go put your pants on and I'll be out shortly. And start the coffee, please."

Michael willingly obeyed. This was definitely a different side of him. It reminded Alyce of a time before children when they would have bantered back and forth in mock dispute over her bossiness before falling into a heap of laughter that would have ended in sweet intimacy. Immediately, the brooding thought of him with another woman overwhelmed Alyce's tiny cloud of nostalgia. She visibly shook her head and climbed out of bed to throw the curtains back, exposing the light.

It was a new day with new hope and mercy.

"What should I do now?" Alyce asked the gorgeous view that lay in front of her.

She became engrossed in watching activity on the beach. There was a young man in khaki shorts and a resort polo busily placing the pairs of royal blue beach chairs on the sand. He had already lined up identical umbrellas, spaced perfectly to follow the curve of the seashore. Now he positioned a chair with precision on either side under the shade of each one.

Alyce thought how the chairs were always placed in pairs, with a big, protective umbrella squarely between them. By day's end, some people would have chosen to move the chair out from under the protection it provided, but that umbrella never moved.

The thought entered her mind that the chairs on the beach could represent marriages. Each umbrella indicated the strong presence of God in the middle. It was there to provide equal covering, as long as the chairs stayed close and remained in its shade. But even if a chair was moved, it could always be moved back. There was nothing blocking it from being placed in perfect order, just as it had begun.

Each pair of chairs had the renter's name written on a card and placed in a pocket on the back. The chairs and umbrellas bore the name of the resort permanently printed in ink.

No matter where on that beach anyone carried a chair, it was still identifiable and able to be returned to its rightful owner, the resort. The name in the pocket helped the renters find their way back to their pair of chairs.

Alyce recalled how sad she'd been on the first day not to have some-one in the other chair marked Keriman, as they were always rented in pairs. That was until Ben came along and joined her the past two days. But his presence in the chair still never matched with the name of the individual who should have been seated there. Ben had been a placeholder. A very pleasant placeholder, but not the rightful owner nonetheless.

Now the rightful owner was here in this very condo with her. Alyce was a jumble of questions and hope contrasted with doubts and despair. She was weary of the roller coaster that had become her life. She had never wanted to get on this ride in the first place. She wondered if it might finally come to an end so she and Michael could get off and return to life together.

Another thought hit her like a swift punch in the gut. Was Michael's appearance just a lull to trick her before the coaster lurched to new heights, plummeting quicker and more violently, leaving Alyce screaming and holding on for dear life? How did she know this wasn't all a part of his crisis?

The thought angered her. A sinister feeling knotted her stomach as she realized how quickly he had stolen her peace. She turned and reached for her gym shorts and tennis shoes. Alyce needed that walk on the beach to calm down. She tied her shoes, yanking the laces so fiercely they could break.

Alyce's every movement seemed controlled by a violent surge of emotion that now propelled her. She'd been at the mercy of the whims of her husband for so long. At times she thought she was losing her mind. Before she'd left home she had purposed that this craziness was not going to ruin her. Not while she sat idly by. Yet here she was again, the familiar waves of nausea growing as the ride began.

She'd never known anyone to jump from a moving roller coaster and survive, but this might be her chance. Whatever Michael was expecting when she threw open the door, his face registered pure shock as she plowed into the living room. He had planned to greet her and offer a cup of coffee, but Alyce marched straight for the door.

She paused and swiveled to meet Michael head-on. Hands on her hips, she announced, "I am a confident, capable woman. I have loved you for a lifetime, but I will not stand by and let you destroy me. I'm not a puppet and I have great value. I won't play games, Michael Keriman. I will not!"

And with that Alyce left. She never even registered Michael's reaction. She skipped the elevator and headed straight for the stairs. Her life had become surreal. She'd wanted adventure and excitement after the kids had gone, but not like this and not on anyone else's terms.

Bursting through the door at the bottom of the stairs, she ran headlong into Ben. She didn't even slow down. She proceeded through the parking garage and didn't stop until she'd reached the open beach. Passing the blue umbrella and chairs marked "Keriman," Alyce stopped, removed one of the cards, and turned it around, stuffing it back in with the blank side showing no name. Today she was solo.

Chapter Seventeen
MICHAEL AND BEN

"*W*ow."

Michael blurted out loud as his wife closed the door behind her. It wasn't a "wow" to indicate "seriously?" as it might have in the past. It was a genuine exclamation of disbelief. He had played out quite a few scenarios of his arrival here in Orange Beach. In each one Alyce was the predictable, serene constant. She would listen to his heart and tell him they would work it all out. This woman who marched through the living room was not familiar.

A knock at the door broke through his thoughts. Michael opened it to find Ben standing there. He stepped aside and gestured as an invitation to come in.

"Alyce just left. I was going to suggest you and I go to the lobby or back to your place, but I don't think she'll be back anytime soon."

Ben had slipped another note under Alyce's door, but this one was addressed to Michael. He had given him his number and asked him to text if he was willing to meet.

"It's nice to officially meet you, Michael. Thanks for agreeing to see me."

"I must confess I'm very off my game here. I came in search of my wife, but I've found someone I don't quite recognize. And, as I see it, she has some sort of relationship with you," Michael said as he motioned for Ben to have a seat on the couch. He, himself, had moved directly across to sit in Alyce's chair.

Ben fidgeted a bit, leaning forward, adjusting his collar, then sitting back and crossing his ankle over his knee. He wiped his forehead. Instinctively, he reached out to still his foot that had begun to shake in time with the pulse racing through his veins.

He had no doubt he was right where God wanted him to be. He couldn't say he was happy about the role he needed to play in Michael's life. Everything in him had wanted to hurry after Alyce when they'd collided in the garage.

But it was apparent being there with Michael was a greater calling. He had spent too much of life looking out for himself. Now he was going to show the ultimate love for Alyce by helping her husband find his way. If possible. How could he even know if Michael would receive what he had to share?

"Let me begin by saying that Alyce and I just met four days ago. We have made a quick connection, that's for sure, but really it has been a friendship that has unfolded. Would I consider the pursuit of something more? I'd be lying to us both to say that wasn't true. To me, she seems worth it."

"Michael, I haven't always been a man of character. I will tell you that my track record with respect to women is nowhere near what it should have been, had I lived by my upbringing and my claim to be a follower of Christ. You have a beautiful, smart, talented wife. She is funny and fun and has one of the purest hearts I've ever known."

It was difficult to read Michael's expression. He appeared almost stoic, in light of all Ben was confessing, but how else could he respond? Ben was an attractive, successful man reiterating everything he knew about his wife. Things he should have been affirming in her for years now. When he moved out of their home, Michael had not seriously expected Alyce to spend the rest of her life pining for him. Or had he? Truthfully, Michael hadn't considered Alyce much at all.

Well, that wasn't entirely true. He *had* thought of Alyce when he thought of his children. He knew they'd be okay, because he relied on Alyce to maintain their normal for them. He had not only abused his personal relationship with Alyce. He had also abused his parenting relationship with Alyce, and thereby jeopardized the relationship with his kids.

During the night, he'd tossed and turned on the sofa, mulling over the discovery of his wife with another man. He was shocked at his hypocrisy when he thought, *What will Maggie, Lillian, and Harrison think?*

Indeed, his own voice mocked him, *what will the children think?* It was a ridiculous notion that Alyce's actions, which he knew would always have been with the most noble intentions, could have been perceived as wrong, considering his own behavior over the past year.

Ben was still and quiet. And praying. Michael had gone somewhere else in his thoughts and Ben's spirit was instructing him to wait. Neither man looked at the other. He waited patiently for some sort of reaction. When Michael spoke, his voice was low.

"I have no right…" He began awkwardly. His voice cracked with emotion. He cleared his throat and began again, trying to summon his courtroom voice.

"I have no right to interfere with Alyce's life anymore," he said. "I have abused and broken vow after vow I made to her. After all she's given me, I have repaid her with neglect and embarrassing behavior. I have forfeited my right to her. I hope you two can be happy together."

Ben wasn't sure whether to be incredulous or feel pity on the poor guy. In the span of a few seconds he prayed for words to come, and they did.

"Michael, I figure we are about the same age. In fact, I believe we originally married our wives around the same time. It wasn't long after our first child, a daughter, was born that I stepped out on my wife, Amie. When she found out, her response wasn't mean or controlling. That's because she was good and kind and everything I was not. We were young and her heart unjaded by my abuse. She gave me grace and agreed to counseling."

"We got better—sadly, she at overlooking my infidelities and I at disguising them. We were two parts of a whole that was very messed up. Her side overcompensated for my side, which was sick and nasty. My side played games all the while. Like a malignancy, it metastasized and ruined everything it touched. When Amie found out she was pregnant with our son, we were basically married on paper only. I moved out and wasn't sure what was next. Then my dad died and I had a 'come to Jesus' moment and went back home."

"See, my dad, while he had his faults, loved his family dearly. He gave us everything he never had and I responded with ungratefulness. I was obsessed with myself. Amie was my high school sweetheart. We were a golden couple all through college. After graduate school, Dad helped me buy out his friend's business and I immediately took it to the next level. Everything came easily to me. I felt invincible. But when he died…"

At this point, Ben was overwhelmed with emotion and paused. It had been a long time since he'd mentioned his father. He wasn't sure he'd ever shared about him as intimately. He regained his composure and forged ahead. By this point, he wasn't talking to Michael as much as merely talking. He was opening old wounds that needed to heal.

"I was repentant, but not to the point of change. I had sorrow over not being the dad my father had been. I had sorrow, because in the deepest part of me, I loved my wife and children. But my appetite for women, for satisfaction, for the next ego trip—however you'd label it—proved greater. Soon, I was in another inappropriate relationship. When Benjamin was born, I almost missed his birth because I was at a hotel with a 'colleague' and had turned off my phone. Can you believe that?"

At this, Ben looked back at Michael for the first time. He hadn't presumed anything when he arrived. He had come out of obedience to the Holy Spirit. Ben had felt forcefully that God wanted him to tell his story, but maybe he needed a filter. Some of it Michael didn't need to know. Would he think Ben was crazy?

Michael was somewhat dumbfounded. He had no intimate friendships with other men. He was not raised to be this personal. His own father rarely shared deep conversation with him, unless it regarded money or business. It was simply not his way. Throughout the years, he and Alyce were very social, but he kept those relationships at a safe distance. Not one of those friends was close enough to confront him when he left his wife. This level of transparency was different.

For some reason, it was not uncomfortable. Rather than becoming anxious about the things Ben shared, he felt empathy for this stranger who had befriended his wife.

"How old is your son?" Michael broke the silence.

"He's fifteen now. My daughter, Nicole, she's eighteen. We have a relationship of sorts. And I keep working at it, because they're my heart. They are terrific kids. Praise God, I didn't completely ruin Amie and she remarried about twelve years ago. Her husband is an amazing father to them. He's taught them all the things I would have."

"That's tough," Michael said. "There's still plenty of life for them to learn from you." He felt a kinship with Ben. Somehow connected, and not just through their reckless choices.

"Why'd you come here, Michael? I mean, Alyce obviously wasn't expecting you."

"I needed to see her. I needed to…I guess I just needed *her*."

Michael looked out at the beach. A teenage boy ran and jumped onto a skimboard, gliding across the water's edge and hopping off just before he crashed. He ran back to his starting point and repeated the process again. Suddenly, Michael was aware that Alyce had entered his view and was also watching the young man. After a few more runs, Alyce engaged the boy in brief conversation before he returned to his board. She proceeded to a set of blue chairs, where she sat and began removing her shoes.

"You know what they say the definition of insanity is? Doing the same thing over and over…"

"And expecting different results," Ben finished for Michael. "I hear you."

Michael said, "I think we had become so predictable, and I was just bored. I had no idea that Alyce was bored, too. I'm not even sure she knew she was bored."

Ben waited. He could tell there was more Michael wanted to say, but needed to process his thoughts. Their silence was comfortable, like two old friends.

When Michael finally spoke, he sounded stronger. "I'm not sure *what* I expect from her. Honestly, I wish we could just get in the car and go home and back in time to before all this began. But then we'd just be bored and together. I suppose that's better than not bored and apart. But surely that isn't all the rest of our lives are meant to be."

"I understand," Ben said. "I think we plan most of our lives when we're in our teens. And for some reason our vision extends right up to about the time we have kids of our own, then we sort of expect it to unfold from there. We never consider that I've got a set of plans and she's got a set of plans. Just because we find each other and fall in love doesn't mean the two plans automatically become one earth-shattering marriage to last forever."

Ben continued, "I don't know about you, but I've done a lot with *my* plans. That's not gone well in most areas of my life. So, now I seek every day to be open to whatever God's got on the agenda. It certainly keeps life interesting."

Michael watched as Alyce walked knee deep into the lapping waves and stood before returning to her chair.

"I don't want to live without her."

"Then don't," Ben said. "From where I sit, I see great promise for you. You'll have to jump some hurdles. You'll have to extend a lot of mercy while she heals. But the good doctor, Luke, said, 'Nothing will be impossible with God.' We've got a great promise right there. I'd lay hold of it and run as far and as fast as I could. Michael, God doesn't want you to love Alyce as best as you can. *He* wants to lavish love on Alyce *through* you. He'll start something new. There's nothing boring about that."

Michael was humbled. He was still confused with how things had rapidly unfolded in recent days. He didn't want Maggie's news and his impending role as grandfather to be his motivation. He honestly didn't want his love for the woman under the blue umbrella to be his motivation. He was just beginning to realize that his love and respect for God was what should move him to repentance.

Michael stood and faced the window. When Ben spoke from right behind him, it startled him. He wasn't aware that Ben had joined him at the window. Together they saw Alyce sitting under the blue umbrella. "Go join her," he said. "You don't want someone else to come along and sit in that other chair."

Chapter Eighteen
MICHAEL AND ALYCE

*I*n all their years of marriage, Alyce could not recall a time she and Michael had ever sat together on the beach. Every year they travelled to the same spot in Florida, renting in the same complex for exactly one week of vacation.

When the kids were young, she'd take them down after breakfast to play in the sand and water while he worked inside. A couple of hours later he'd come out to play while Alyce prepared lunch.

A quick poolside picnic was followed by Alyce taking Maggie, Lillian, and Harrison up for a nap. Michael would sit outside and read a book or magazine while she tidied up and read indoors as the children slept. This was their routine.

After naps, there might be time for more swimming before everyone was dressed and headed out for dinner. Inevitably, the sun and the surf always worked to make the kids ready for an early bedtime, for which they were both grateful. The two of them would read or watch a movie before turning in. Alyce was usually quite exhausted herself.

As the children became teenagers, they were allowed to bring friends along. More work for her, but Alyce thoroughly enjoyed it. Michael typically would drive the boy car, following Alyce with her carload of girls. During those years she was a short-order cook and laundress the entire trip, but she didn't mind. It wouldn't last for long and they'd be grown. She loved the laughter and the game nights. The random hugs from Harrison's gangly basketball buddies and the nights when the girls let her hang out in their room and listen to their chatter.

Two summers ago, Maggie was a newlywed and Lillian was studying abroad. Michael bought himself a Jeep Wrangler hardtop convertible, strictly for the beach. Maybe he was trying to recapture a little of his lost youth, but she secretly thought he was satisfying a need to be the cool dad. It didn't bother her. Alyce, without her own car companions, still drove in order to accommodate the food and beach toys for the boys. That year Harrison was allowed to bring three friends. They all rode with Michael in the Jeep.

Harrison had just gotten his license and was ecstatic over his dad's splurge. He and his buddies couldn't wait to drive it along the strip at night. Enjoying the Jeep on summer vacation would be short lived, but fun for the two summers before Harrison headed to college. She wondered if Michael had considered offering it to Harrison for spring break with his fraternity brothers this year.

She never understood why they only drove the Jeep on vacation. Otherwise, it sat in the extra garage where Michael would periodically crank it or take it on errands. It would have been fantastic to drive on the Trace when the fall leaves were at peak or on a summer night to get ice cream. Alyce had imagined such things for the two of them, but they never happened.

She would have enjoyed a tropical vacation with her husband. Over the years they could have gone, but she'd never brought it up, because she knew it was part of the long-range plan. Something they looked forward to one day, but one day never came.

Very early in their marriage, there had been the occasional legal conference when they had slipped away to Savannah or San Diego. Even with his structured itinerary, Michael would find time for sightseeing. They stayed in beautiful hotels and ate amazing meals.

Once Maggie was born, neither of them wanted to leave the children with grandparents for more than an overnight sleepover. Alyce's trips with Michael were put on hold. In spite of their plan to resume travels when the kids started school, that day just never arrived. Alyce and Michael developed a system for his conference trips. He would only be gone for a night, two nights max, leaving her to keep an eye on things around the house. They convinced themselves it was for the best and just a season in life. They had big plans for after the children were gone.

Alyce was deep in these thoughts when Michael appeared and took the seat beside her under the blue umbrella. The seat that didn't have his name on it. She barely acknowledged his presence as he settled in, then leaned back and closed her eyes. He was rather comical, still dressed in his dress pants and shirt. He had removed his socks and shoes and rolled his pants legs, exposing the whitest legs she believed she'd ever seen. She wondered why in the world he hadn't changed his clothes.

The walk had helped her mood, but welcoming Michael into her sanctuary was a big deal. She hoped not to surrender her recomposed tranquility and peace of mind.

Minutes passed. Alyce snuck a peek at him. He had focused on the horizon, seemingly deep in thought. She, too, found a boat in the distance and locked her gaze on the small craft. She had no idea how long they sat there.

At last Michael glanced her way, and seeing she was no longer resting her eyes, said, "Alyce, I'm sorry."

"Is that why you're here?" Alyce turned toward him and calmly asked. "Just to say you're sorry?"

"I'm here because I screwed up in a really big way and I know I don't deserve it, but I'd like for you to forgive me."

"You need my forgiveness? I did that a long time ago, Michael." Alyce's tone was dismissive. Not a drop of cordiality crept into her tone.

"Okaaayyy...," Michael drug it out. "What do you mean?"

"You should know me well enough to know that I've never been one for grudges and I don't like the way it feels when I'm angry. You didn't have to ask to receive it. But thank you for asking."

They both resumed their forward gaze and sat quietly.

"It's really nice here," Michael said, sounding like one who had discovered something new and unique.

"Yes. Yes, it is," Alyce replied. "It may very well be my new favorite place."

"I had trouble finding you."

"How *did* you find me, Michael? I didn't even tell the kids where I'd be. I told Maggie before I left that if they needed me I could be reached by phone, but otherwise I wanted to be off the grid. The kids knew I was safe. I don't understand how you figured it out." Alyce was now talking more with herself than to Michael. "I don't even think I wrote anything down, except when Salli called with the name and number..." Suddenly, Alyce exclaimed, "Michael, have you been in my house?"

Michael winced at her reference to "my" house. The sound of it made him sad and sick at the same time. Why *shouldn't* he be in their home? He knew the answer, and yet he hated admitting that he was the reason.

Alyce interrupted his thoughts. "If you think you're going to leave me, set up residence in a new place with another woman, and still come and go as you please in *my* home—the only place I can rightfully claim as safe territory—you've officially lost it!"

With that she stood and stomped into the water. Dang it! The roller-coaster car lurched upward. She longed to dive in and swim away, wishing she'd taken the time to put on her swimsuit under her shorts and T-shirt. Surprisingly, Michael was hot on her heels, following her into the shallow surf. He looked ridiculous as he held his pants legs higher. Nevertheless, they randomly dipped in and out with each wave.

"I did go in the house."

Michael avoided saying 'your' or 'our' when referencing their home.

"I wasn't rational and I knew it was wrong. I admit that, okay? You could have me arrested for breaking and entering," he said with a slight tease in his voice.

He hoped the comment might serve to lighten the mood. It did not. Alyce stood firmly with her arms folded, refusing to make eye contact.

"I cannot express to you how low I had gotten."

She pivoted and snidely replied, "Oh yes, I know that *very* well."

"Not *that* kind of low," Michael said. "I was broken and sad and lonely and depressed. That's why I entered the house. I wanted to find you. To know where you were so I could *be* with you. I need you, Alyce, more than anything in this world. I need you and more than that, I *want* you!" With that declaration, Michael reached to grab her hand.

Alyce snatched it away and stomped from the water. Gathering her shoes she headed toward the pool. Michael was undeterred. He followed her every step, talking the entire way.

"I'm not sure what I will have to do to make this right. But I can tell you that I will die trying. I miss everything about you, Alyce. I miss your smile and your humor. I miss that crazy way you pour out my glass of tea before I'm done with it. I miss your smell and the way you move through a room. I *love* you and I have broken every promise I ever made to you. I mean, what kind of human being *does* that to another? I must have been outside my mind."

Alyce continued to walk briskly, although she was no longer stomping. He sounded shockingly sincere, but he had sounded sincere for the entire twenty-six years they'd been married. According to the Michael she knew last week, all those years had been a lie.

She was so mad at him. A fury that had bubbled and boiled for months was dangerously close to spilling over. Until now, she'd not let him see her this angry over him. It was not Alyce's nature to be angry. She didn't know what to do. Rage was foreign, but seemed a response Michael was intent on dragging out of her, whether through his flagrant infidelity or his flip-flop of rhetoric.

Prickly needles of irritation tingled up and down her arms, and in that moment all she could hear was the voice of her Southern mama saying, "Somebody's always watching you." That one statement could send her into a tailspin. *I don't care!* she wanted to scream. *Let people stare! They have no right to judge me. It's none of their business!* Subconsciously, Alyce made fists and flexed her fingers while digging her fingernails into the palms of her hands.

She had reached the pool area and glanced around at the few people there, almost daring them to look her way. Her drama was unfolding in broad daylight for all to see. If they were nervy enough to look, she was not accountable for her response. Lucky for them, no one even noticed her arrival on the scene. They seemed intent on their own tasks. Alyce guessed the voice of her mother was only there to needle her further.

If Michael *wasn't* sincere, his timing was maddening. A perfectly wonderful man was somewhere close by. Finding such companionship was something she would have never predicted, much less so soon. She had told herself it didn't matter if she ever had that kind of relationship again. *Why is this happening to me?* Alyce prayed accusingly. *I was quite content with my plan to live in peace as a single woman.*

A voice inside her head responded, *Ben could do this to you, too. He basically confessed so himself. Why are you willing to give credibility to a man you've known a few days and not to this man you've known for a lifetime?*

Alyce stopped in her tracks. It was all unfair. This was not her choosing. Her resolve was flailing wildly.

"Michael, stop talking!" Alyce pivoted as she thrust her hand in his direction, keeping him at a distance. Without looking at him she asked, "Tell me, when did you have this revelation?"

They were now standing directly beside the pool. Thankfully, it wasn't crowded. A college boy in a resort shirt skimmed the surface of the water for bugs. A young mother helped her toddler put on his swimmies while the older sister sat patiently on the steps.

The sight of the mother with her children made Alyce soften. She wanted to help the young woman and have a casual conversation about potty training and naps. She did not want to be talking about what *had* happened and what *could* happen and how very *sorry* Michael was at that moment.

None of that mattered. All the old weariness she had carried since learning of Michael's affair crept up and over her back, threatening to consume her soul. She had felt so rested and at peace the last two days. Now the complications of divorce and affairs and broken promises and angry children pressed in with more fervor than ever before.

She closed her eyes and visualized the darkness thrusting its arms deep into her innermost being. The vicelike squeeze threatened to suffocate her. A cloying feeling she'd forgotten threatened to choke her. Like a ripe tomato on the hottest day of the summer, Alyce felt she was one degree away from splitting wide open and spilling all over the pool deck.

She thought the walk on the beach had allowed her to regain composure, but now she was teetering between a total meltdown and murdering her husband. Alyce was not a violent woman, but she found herself wanting to use her fists to pound Michael's chest repeating, *What. is. wrong. with. you. You. are. so. weird.* with every blow.

All the while, Michael was still talking, "We can go to counseling. Let me move back in...I'll live in another bedroom," he offered.

He stopped when he saw the look on Alyce's face. It somewhat scared him, because it reminded him of the time a kid at school had spread rumors about one of their children. He knew his wife wanted to hurt someone. He took one step back, then two steps toward her.

"Alyce? Are you okay?"

In one fell swoop, Alyce stepped into Michael's space declaring, "No, I most definitely am not!" She shoved with both hands, pushing him squarely into the water. It felt good, but wasn't nearly enough. Alyce was an amateur at anger and it was the best she had, but it did strangely little to alleviate the tension that had coiled her insides.

She intentionally relaxed her hands and squared her shoulders, stretching her fingers down by her sides as if willing the tension to flow from the tips. Taking a deep breath, she turned and walked around the pool to the pathway leading inside. She passed the young mother who looked at her rather benignly. At first it seemed odd, but then maybe she, too, had wished she could push someone in the pool that very morning.

Alyce felt Mr. Hyde subside as Dr. Jekyll reemerged in sympathy to the young woman handling the two children alone. The mom smiled at Alyce as the little girl waved from her perch on the top step. Alyce acted as if everything were normal, and she was oblivious of the fully clothed man sputtering and splashing in the deep end. She waved back.

"Your children are precious. Enjoy every minute," she said rounding the end of the pool.

Michael was floored by Alyce's behavior, but impressed. As he bobbed to the top and regained his composure, a weird grin came over his face. He shouted after Alyce, "I still love you!"

Alyce was unmoved, but the young mother was now watching the entire saga as she eased her little boy into the water. Michael was walking through the shallow end toward the steps and as he passed her he patted the little guy on his head and said, "Maybe one day you'll have a wonderful woman in your life just like that one."

And with that he walked out of the pool and toward the garage to find his car, his suitcase, and some dry clothes. This new Alyce intrigued him. He determined he would not let her go. Stopping beside a palm tree, Michael held on as he squeezed the water from the bottom of his pant leg. He felt something inside he hadn't in a long while, and it was amazing.

Chapter Nineteen

BEN AND ALYCE

*A*lyce did not expect to encounter Ben in the garage. He was loading a box of groceries and a beach chair into the back of his Range Rover. She could plainly see his suitcases already arranged inside the open hatch.

"Were you planning to leave without saying goodbye?" she tossed at him. She sounded angry, but she wasn't. Actually, she realized she *was* angry. Ben appeared unfazed by her tone and warmly responded.

"Just getting a start on loading since it's my day to head home. I have to be out of the condo by eleven. But I wouldn't leave without knowing you're okay."

"Why *wouldn't* I be okay?" Alyce snapped. "Everything is just peachy and I haven't a care in the universe. Why in the world wouldn't I be *ecstatic*? My husband, whom I don't even want to *call* my husband, has spent the past year telling me I'm crazy every time I accused him of lying to me, while, might I add, lying the entire time, and assuring me I'm not now nor have I ever really been what he wants, and created a life with a younger woman, thereby alienating our children and aging me by *at least* ten years. Now he is suddenly here, looking dejected and all *please let's make this work?*" Alyce's voice echoed in the parking garage. "I am perfectly, ridiculously, gloriously better than okay. I am *smashing*!"

Alyce gestured wildly and accentuated the last three words by poking the air with her finger. In reality, she wished she had a baseball bat and could break the windows in every single car around her. There was a word that described how she felt. Why was it eluding her? Alyce snapped her fingers and shook her head. She knew exactly what it was. She was livid!

Ben appeared unmoved by her antics. He finished loading his car, then pushed the button to close the door. "Let's go," he said as he gently took her arm and guided her to the passenger side. Alyce allowed herself to be placed in the seat as her mind tossed wild thoughts around like clothes tumbling in a dryer. Ben swiftly walked around and slid into the driver's side, cranked the car, and backed out of his space.

He was sweating from his labors and punched the max button on the AC as he turned onto the main road. Quietly and patiently, he rode in silence beside Alyce, who vacillated between chewing her lip and patting her foot violently, then pounding her fingers up and down on the edges of her seat. The wheels spinning in her head were almost visible. He knew she would exhaust herself and waited for her to regain composure before even attempting a conversation.

Ben hadn't eaten since dinner the previous night and he assumed neither had Alyce. His hunch was confirmed when he heard her stomach growl. She was oblivious to it all, until she realized he had stopped the car

Looking around, Alyce exclaimed, "Waffle House? Seriously?"

"It's the best place for breakfast and for sorting through life," Ben said. "I love Waffle House and I'm buying so I get to choose. Besides, your stomach's been growling the entire ride here." Alyce instinctively placed her hand on her stomach.

He popped his seatbelt and opened the door. Pausing mid-exit, he turned and asked, "You coming?"

Alyce inhaled deeply and exhaled slowly. Her blood pressure was likely through the roof, so why not add in some greasy, artery-clogging grub? At that very moment, she thought what a relief it would be to just step on out of this life and be at the feet of Jesus. *Even better*, she thought, *LORD, why don't You just come for all of us?* Alyce reluctantly opened her door.

They had barely settled into a booth when the waitress appeared. Her cheery disposition was a momentary distraction from the silence and moodiness Alyce had to offer. Alyce classified Waffle House servers in the same category as bartenders. They gave her the feeling they knew things about life no one else did. Waffle House employees were endowed with super powers to rush in with more than a hearty breakfast in lightning speed. They also seemed to always have the right attitude. It was as though their job description included, *Must have wisdom to provide practical perspective to every situation.*

Ben ordered them both coffees and waters and as the server—who said her name was Tricia if they needed anything—walked away, he placed his forearms on the table and leaned in. Ben looked Alyce in the eyes and gave her a gentle, knowing smile.

"What?" Alyce asked. His scrutiny irritated her. She wasn't sure anything anyone did at that moment was going to be right. He knew this, too, so he figured he had nothing to lose.

"Tell me what has been at the forefront of your prayers the past nine months." Ben spoke gently, but matter-of-factly.

"I don't know…" Alyce's impatient response trailed. Her frustration dulled. She tried to follow his meaning. Where was he going with this?

"Think about what has occupied your every waking moment and interrupted your sleep. What have you talked to God about? Journaled about?"

Alyce leaned back, away from Ben's probing blue eyes. In that moment, they held none of their previous intrigue, but they still offered something Alyce longed to accept. Kindness. A genuine desire to be her friend. Alyce felt her shoulders relax slightly and allowed herself to engage his warmth.

"I suppose it's been to pray for my children."

"And?"

"I've prayed for wisdom to know what to do about my marriage."

"And?"

"I wish I knew what you are looking for. Help me out, please?"

Tricia arrived, balancing two cups of coffee and two glasses of water. "Cream?" she asked.

"Yes, please," Alyce said, welcoming the lull in the conversation while Tricia retrieved a bowl of individual creamers. She whipped a pad from her apron and asked if they were ready to order.

"What's the most popular?" she asked as Tricia grinned and hollered a greeting to a regular who walked in the door.

"Oh, that'd be the All-star," Tricia said, leaning in to tap her pencil at the picture on the laminated menu. "A waffle, hash browns, two eggs, toast, and your choice of bacon, ham, or sausage."

Ben leaned back. "That's what I'm having! Eggs scrambled. Hash browns scattered, smothered and covered. Plain toast, not the raisin kind. And could I get country ham instead of city?"

Tricia scribbled on her pad. "You got it! And for you ma'am?"

Alyce was speechless. Finally, gesturing toward Ben she said, "I'll have the same."

Tricia turned and reeled off their entire order for the whole restaurant to hear. An older gentleman moved around the cooktop like an artist, pulling pans and ladling oil as he cracked eggs and shifted massive amounts of meat around the grill. All while popping four pieces of bread into a toaster and serving up plates to be delivered to tables down the way. The waffle irons were hot and working to capacity.

"I guess everyone here now knows that I'm having a huge breakfast," Alyce said, still irritable.

Ben laughed and asked, "What are the rest of these folks having?"

Alyce quipped, "I don't know. I was too preoccupied with your quiz to hear."

"Precisely," Ben said. "We all think everyone's engaged in our lives, while we rarely know what's going on in theirs. Own your decisions and live the way you deem best. Truth is, no one is as interested in your drama as you think. They're too busy with their own." Alyce sat in silence while she processed his sensible answer.

"Whatever you said," she responded with a shrug. "What are we doing here? *Besides* having breakfast," she added before he could supply a snarky response.

Ben was anything but snarky. He was attempting to draw her out of her anger and into a healthy discussion of the matters at hand. Last night a little part of her had hoped he'd kiss her. Today she wanted to smack him. Pushing Michael into the pool was not enough to satisfy the adrenaline rushing through her body. She couldn't decide if it was rage or anxiety. She only knew it was not the desired outcome of a week at the beach.

"Your prayers," Ben said as he opened one blue packet and poured it into his coffee. "What would you say has been at the forefront of them in recent months? Particularly right after Michael moved out." Ben pulled back the tab on a creamer and emptied its contents into the cup. Alyce watched the black liquid turn a lighter brown as he swirled it all together with his spoon.

"I guess that he'd come back to me."

Ben nudged the bowl of creamer, coaxing her to prepare her own cup. She reached for a sweetener and two creamers. Neither of them spoke until she had finished and lifted the warm, comforting cup to her lips.

"And would you say that God is now attempting to answer that prayer?"

Alyce set down the mug and looked at Ben. Of course. But she had to admit she'd been praying without hope for so long that perhaps they were prayers of obligation. Had Michael returned immediately, they would have gone to counseling, addressed the infidelity, and moved on with life.

As the months passed, however, much more was revealed about herself as well as her husband. Things about his character and who she had become. Her prayers never changed one bit regarding his return, but now that possibility appeared to be a greater challenge than she'd anticipated. In the growing fatigue of waiting, she'd begun to pray a rote prayer.

It was no longer a simple matter of him coming home and them resuming life as they'd known it. Everything—*everything*—had changed. So now she faced the potential of an answered prayer, unprepared to deal with the enormity of that answer.

Alyce had convinced herself that God was asleep on this matter. Or confused. Or incompetent, if she was honest. So, perhaps she had decided He wouldn't answer and, therefore, no longer prepared herself to receive her request.

"Okay, Mr. Wise One, where are we going with this line of questioning?"

"You have prayed for this day for a long time. You have agonized over the simple issue of Michael returning home. You've poked and prodded your marriage, trying to determine areas where it needed propping up and others where it all seemed fine to you. But somewhere in the recesses of that complicated brain, you've relied on the fact that, if Michael would just return home, everything would be alright. When it wasn't alright before he ever left."

He dared not pause, so he forged ahead.

"Pardon my intrusion into your thought process, but I'd bet money you had already given up on his return and had begun preparations for life without him. Physically and emotionally. You'd begun a cleaning out of sorts to rid yourself of lingering expectations for any kind of future that resembled your original plan when you said, 'I do.' "

"You were preparing the burial plot when there was not yet a corpse, you were so convinced that death was imminent. I don't blame you. I'm just making observations. I have experience with this, remember."

Alyce furrowed her brow. She was at a loss for words. Ben paused for her to speak, then, seeing her struggle, continued.

"This is not going to be easy, Alyce. But Michael loves you. He genuinely does. He's still sort of selfish, but that's okay, considering he completely lost his mind for a minute there."

He raised his hands in surrender at her expression. "I know. I know it has seemed like a lifetime. He allowed himself to follow his flesh to places he never should have gone, and because you two are one, he took you with him. He was duped into believing it didn't directly affect you, but I told him some things to show him otherwise and, I think, open his eyes even more."

"You talked to Michael?" Alyce asked, dumbfounded.

"I did. I needed to tell him that this life you two have made together is irreplaceable. He'll never get the chance to recreate something so memorable and encompassing such history with another human being."

"But I don't know if I even want to try any longer. This separation showed me some things about myself and about him that I hadn't noticed before. As of right now, I feel zero love toward him. Zero. His selfish rejection of me after so many attempts at reconnecting has done its job of pushing me completely away. How would I ever find it in my heart to pursue him again? Earlier, on the beach, he touched my hand and it made my skin crawl." Alyce gave a little shudder. "It may be time to just walk away."

"Alyce, why did you pray so hard and ask God to bring him home?"

"Because I loved him at the time. I loved our life and our family and what I thought we had."

"But it was a lie. It was all a part of the roles you two had assumed—neither of you loved life, but you were in a comfortable place together that was slowly killing you both. An affair is an awful, terrible thing to have happen, but it has reawakened in you guys a realization that you originally wanted more when you began. I want you to resume that dream together. You were once on your way. You can have it again."

"I just don't know," Alyce placed her face in her hands. She squeezed her eyes tightly shut and shook her head viciously. "Why are you saying all of this to me?" She looked straight at him, "I thought we were beginning our own friendship."

"We were. We *are*. Friends, that is. Two folks who need what the other can offer, but in the truest sense of the word friendship. In another time and place, we could have pursued more. But my role in this situation is to be a voice of reason and rationale for you and Michael both. I enjoyed talking with him this morning. He's a nice guy."

Tricia arrived and began setting plates of food on the table. So many plates! One plate for waffles and one for bacon. One with eggs and hash browns. Another with toast. Alyce's head was down and she followed

Tricia's every movement with intense interest. With a promise to return shortly with more coffee, Tricia placed a small pitcher of syrup between them and left.

Ben looked across at Alyce to find her gaze fixed on the sweet, brown liquid. Tears pooled in her eyes. He knew when she blinked they would spill. The look on her face was one of hopelessness and despair. Had he gone too far?

"Alyce?" he ventured.

"No one wants me. I'm no good to anyone." She didn't move, but spoke in a somber monotone.

"What?" Ben exclaimed in total disbelief. "Where did you get that idea?"

"I'm Michael's choice simply because I'm safe for him. I provide stability and comfort. Now that he's had his little fling we can quietly finish out our lives together. Back to things as they were and a miserable existence I didn't even recognize a year ago."

Ben was still trying to process when she continued, "And you don't want me. You probably see me the same way now, since he's painted a picture of who I am to him. Predictable, reliable Alyce," she said in a singsong voice. "My children don't need me. I'm the safe choice for Michael. He rode the roller coaster; now he's back to his old, familiar seat on the merry-go-round."

Ben would have laughed at the last comment, had he not been completely flabbergasted. It had been a while since he'd dealt with female emotions from someone he cared about. And he cared deeply for Alyce. She was an amazing person who had survived an incredibly rough season. He wanted to protect her, even though they'd only just met.

Alyce picked up the tiny Waffle House napkin and dabbed at her eyes, attempting to stem the tide before it overcame her.

"Why do they give you such tiny little scraps to use?" she lamented.

She was thankful she hadn't put on makeup before her walk on the beach. That seemed like an eternity ago. Alyce was weary. So, so weary.

Her sorrow had been carefully packed away for months now. There was no time for sadness. She had to be the cheerleader for her children, the champion for her family, and the "good face" for all their friends.

When she arrived at the beach, the plan had been to unpack her heartaches, slowly, one box at a time, sorting through and healing. Alone. But the distractions of the past few days with Ben had buoyed her hope and made her believe that perhaps she wouldn't have to unpack them at all.

Now, sitting right there in the Waffle House, it felt as though someone had drug out each one and dumped the contents onto the table. Any minute now, Tricia would arrive and begin announcing them for all to hear. It was more than she could bear. She felt an audible sob beginning to build from deep in her chest. It was fighting against the tightly-wound grief that squeezed her like a vise. But she knew the ugliest cry ever on the planet was about to begin. Alyce clamped her hand over her mouth and bolted from the restaurant.

About that time, Tricia did arrive with a smile and a piping hot pot of coffee. "Refills?" she asked, looking at Ben. He shook his head, pulled two $20 bills from his wallet and, tossing them on the table, followed his devastated friend outside.

Ben looked around, but all he could see was a skinny, older woman with bleached hair. She was very tan and wrinkled from years in the sun, walking a Chihuahua in a neatly mowed area beside the parking lot. She wore bright pink pants and an even brighter floral top. As he approached his car, he realized the puppy was a cover for her to smoke. She took a long draw from an even longer cigarette. He considered asking if she'd seen Alyce, but decided against it. Ben felt certain he'd locked his vehicle, but wanted to check the back seat just in case. She was not inside.

Scanning the small lot, he found no trace of Alyce. Where could she have gone? He walked toward the main road to see if she'd begun walking back. Surely not. But then, desperate women did desperate things. He had just turned to walk back to his car when he heard a pitiful, guttural wail from the far side of the building.

Rounding the corner, he found an empty lot where the grass was tall and weedy. He stood still to listen. Again, there came the sound of wailing and anguish. He knew she was somewhere close by.

"Alyce?" Ben called out.

"Go away! Just leave me here," came the angry reply. Promptly on its heels came a loud blubbering, the likes of which Ben had never heard. Where was she?

He took a few more steps and stopped to listen again. Surveying the empty lot, he saw where some of the grass was bent, he presumed under the weight of Alyce's footsteps. He carefully followed them, scanning every which way for some sign of his friend. He nearly tripped over her sitting on the ground grasping her ankle.

"My word, woman!" Ben exclaimed. "What in the Sam Hill are you doing here on the ground?"

"I stepped in a hooooole!" Alyce wailed as loudly as Ben had ever heard.

He was aware that if anyone passing saw the two of them and heard her cries, they would think he was abusing her. Thankfully there was no one in sight, and he knew the woman with the long cigarette couldn't hear them for the sounds of passing traffic. Not that she would care.

Ben squatted in the tall grass and surveyed the situation. This was, as his mother used to say, quite the pickle. It appeared that Alyce's ankle was sprained. It was already turning blue and had begun to swell.

"You can just leave me. I'll figure out something."

Alyce was beyond irrational and beginning to border on annoying. Ben's patience was wearing thin. He was sympathetic as the day was long, but there were limits.

He extended his hand and said, "Let me help you up."

Alyce looked at his hand, sniffed and turned away.

"I'm not really asking. I'm not leaving you here and you can't go it alone on that ankle. So now," he said more forcefully, "let me help you up." He grabbed her elbows and with one fell swoop, Alyce was off the ground and in his secure hold. She hobbled for a second, attempting to stand without him, but when her foot touched the ground she yelped in pain and grabbed him tightly to steady herself. Rather than feeling rescued, Alyce felt ridiculous as she sheepishly looked up at him and said, "I think it might be bad."

Ben repositioned himself, balancing her all the while, and placed his arm around Alyce's waist. Together they made their way back to the parking lot. With each step her foot bobbled, causing her to wince in pain. Ben slipped his hand under her knee to offer more support.

The older woman was taking a long draw from her cigarette and barely looked up when they approached his car. Ben slid Alyce into the passenger seat, intending to drive back to the resort, but Alyce's face was almost white from pain and the swelling was quite impressive. He asked Chihuahua lady if she knew where the closest walk-in clinic might be.

It appeared this was the first question she'd been asked in a long while. She furrowed her brow and pursed her brightly painted red lips. She twisted them to the side as if that might help her think. Then she sniffed and licked her front teeth, making a clucking sound. She drew in a dramatic breath and gesturing left said, "You go out here and turn right, you see? And go down until you see the Dollar General about three miles. Across the street is the Hair You Are salon—it's the purple building. You can't miss it. You'll need to turn left there at that red light.

Go down a little way and there will be a big sign," at this she held her hands out widely in illustration. Ashes dropped from her cigarette as she continued, "that says 'Walk-In Clinic.' You don't want to go there. I went there last year and they said it was just a cold, but I sure enough had the pneumonia before it was all over with! They can't tell a heart attack from an ingrown toenail. Why, my friend Millie…"

Ben raised his hand and interrupted, "Ma'am, it's a bit of an emergency if you don't mind."

Chihuahua lady paused mid-gesture, as if considering whether to continue her story or redirect. She sniffed again, straightened her shoulders, and spoke in an offended voice, "Well, two blocks past the walk-in clinic you will find the hospital. I recommend you take her to the emergency room there."

"Thank you so much. Your poodle is lovely. I mean puppy," Ben said as he slipped behind the steering wheel and quickly backed out, praying her directions to the hospital were accurate. The thought of using the maps on his phone never crossed his mind. Glancing over at Alyce, he knew the ER was the way to go.

Chapter Twenty

ALYCE / BEN / MICHAEL

*T*he emergency room attendant attempted to put Alyce in a wheelchair, but after an initial check of her ankle decided on a gurney for better elevation. She and Ben were now in a bay in the ER, which was merely a room created by curtains on four sides. She had been quiet ever since Ben had helped her to the car at the Waffle House. He wondered if this was her way of handling pain.

Truth be told, she was spent from all the emotion and despondent at the turn of events from the past twenty-four hours. To say she was disappointed in her own reaction was an understatement. Outwardly, Alyce appeared quiet. Inwardly, she and the LORD were having a dandy of a discussion. She measured her surrender by her responses. Today's measurement was not in her favor.

She'd always been a bit dramatic. But the ups and downs of the past nine months had grown Alyce exponentially in handling her emotions. There was nothing like the freedom of learning to surrender her drama to the LORD. She knew she'd been a gross disappointment to Him as she'd snatched control and had a field day with her anger in spite of their sweet communion just that morning.

The words of her dear, Southern Aunt Claudia came to mind. She was always crafting deliciousness in the kitchen and was far too busy to waste words. Something in the way she spoke to her heavenly Father throughout the day made faith tangible rather than some Jesus-in-the-sky, sweet-by-and-by, Sunday school lesson.

Alyce learned that God was accessible through her aunt's down-to-earth relationship with Him. She longed for Aunt Claudia's kitchen now, where she could bare her soul and have a healthy piece of practical perspective along with a slice of ten-layer chocolate cake.

She knew just what Aunt Claudia would tell her today. She would wipe her hands on her apron and stop to put her warm, cinnamon-scented hands on either side of Alyce's face. That was how she said God likes to talk to us so He knows we're listening. She'd say, "You know, baby, when Satan knocks on your door, you can always call out, 'Jesus, will You get that, please and thank You?' He will! And that old snake cannot get in unless you open the door to him. He will overpower you! But not our Warrior! He'll likely run when he hears that Name! Now you go on and let Him fight your battles."

God wanted her surrendered to His will and trusting His love for her, of this she was certain. Nothing in her life had ever caught Him off guard and that was a fact that would never change. When Satan came knocking around her door, she had every right as a daughter of the King to pause and say LORD, *will You get that please and thank You?* The past year had been an advanced course for this practice. Today, Alyce felt like a D student.

Although she knew in her gut God was right there, it felt like all hell had been let loose inside of her. In truth, she couldn't give Satan much credit for it. This was mostly all Alyce Keriman flesh rising and demanding attention. She had hoped that the worst of her emotional extremes were forever behind her. Why would she take control now that she had experienced the peace of surrender?

The words in Hebrews 12:11 played through Alyce's mind. *No discipline seems pleasant at the time, but painful. Later on, however, it produces a harvest of righteousness and peace for those who have been trained by it.*

She really wanted to be angry at Michael for triggering such a reaction. Of course, he was not alone in this. Ben had said plenty to set her off. But if she were honest, neither of them had the power to evoke such a meltdown now that she'd known the power in surrendering circumstances to God. She had to own the fact that she still struggled with complete surrender of everything in her life.

Her anger subsided. Anger had no place in a life of peace. Peace always came when she was quiet and still before the LORD. *Thank You, LORD, for being honest with me and not letting me settle for anything less than Your perfect peace.*

The explosive emotions were spent. Maybe now, after her confrontation with Michael earlier in the day and her nuclear reaction at the Waffle House, she would never again have to confront such extremes. Maybe? Alyce doubted it. Dying to self was a process, and she was more aware of that than ever before.

"I don't understand why Michael isn't answering his phone," Ben broke the silence.

"I didn't know you were trying to reach him. I'm pretty sure it's probably not working," she said. "I think his phone got wet this morning."

"Well that would explain a lot. I wonder if I could call the resort and have them get in touch with him. I'm sure he's worried sick about you."

Alyce didn't respond. When he looked at her, she had closed her eyes to rest. Ben slipped into the hallway and dialed the front desk of the resort.

"Thank you for calling Pelican Pointe. This is Scarlett. How may I direct your call?"

After explaining who he was, Ben attempted to further explain what he needed. *How does one ask for a man who is loitering around the resort?* He described him as best he could, but he wasn't the most observant guy on the planet. He briefly considered asking Alyce to remember what Michael was wearing, but decided against disturbing her.

"Sir," Scarlett spoke in low tones. He imagined her peeking over her cupped hand, eyes darting furtively, as she shielded her end of the conversation. "There's actually a gentleman sitting here in the lobby who may match your description, although it is somewhat vague. He has been asking about one of our guests and insists that he's her husband. He appears to have resigned himself to waiting on her return. Our security detail is keeping a close watch."

"That's him!" Ben exclaimed, then lowered his own voice. "Is there a chance I might speak with him?"

Scarlett put him on hold and walked to where Michael was sitting. Earlier, he had come in from the pool, hoping to find Alyce in the garage. He wasn't deterred when she wasn't there. He couldn't remember ever seeing her so angry. He guessed she'd gone to her room.

After knocking loudly for several minutes at Alyce's door, Michael decided she must be in the shower. Wisdom, and the fact that he had no key, told him to give her time and space to cool down. He thought it best to utilize the spa to shower and send his clothes to the laundry. He had left the keys to his rental car in the condo, so he couldn't access his suitcase. Perhaps he could get a neck massage while he waited for his things to dry. This would give Alyce ample time alone.

Michael had learned this was essential to Alyce's state of mind, coming aside to think and pray. It was a discipline he lacked, or, truthfully, had avoided. Sin rarely seeks repose.

Now he sat in the lobby of the resort. He had attempted to get Alyce to the door once more since drying out in the spa. His phone had taken a devastating bath in the pool. The front-desk attendant should have been employed with the CIA, so guarded was she with any information. He was grateful she hadn't been on duty the previous night when he arrived. He might never have found Alyce. He was growing desperate when he looked up to see her walking toward him. He prayed it wasn't to escort him out.

"Sir?" Scarlett approached him. "Is your name Michael Keriman?" When Michael confirmed that it was so, she continued, "There's a gentleman on the phone who would like to speak with you."

Finally! Maybe it was someone with answers. Michael immediately grew concerned and walked right on her heels, which were very high and refused to move swiftly across the wood floor. She rounded the desk and pushed a button, handing him the receiver.

"Hello, this is Michael Keriman."

"Hey! It's Ben! Thank goodness I've found you. Can you grab a ride and come to Beachside Regional emergency room? Alyce is fine, but she's injured herself and she needs you."

"Yes, of course! Tell me the hospital name again?" he asked while motioning for a pen and paper. He jotted a few things, then said, "Ben, please tell Alyce that I love her and I'm on my way." Without waiting for an answer, he hung up the phone and headed to the valet to call a car.

Ben put his phone in his pocket. He pushed his fingers up through his curly hair. This vacation had proven to be most memorable. The guys would never believe all that had transpired after they left.

He peeked through a crack in the curtain. Alyce seemed so helpless lying there. She needed to let someone help her, yet she'd learned to manage on her own for the past few months. Her newfound independence was not going to be easily relinquished. She held it closely, like a hard-won trophy after a grueling competition. He understood. He recognized that same determination from his own experiences with Amie.

Ben stepped through the curtain and watched Alyce resting. He breathed a prayer for her—a prayer for wisdom and discernment regarding all that Michael's appearance might mean in her life. He prayed that she would be strong and that her truth would come from the LORD and not some chick-flick idea of what a jilted woman's demands should be.

Alyce opened her eyes and looked over at him with a smile on her face. The medicine was working its magic. Alyce actually didn't handle meds very well. Often their effect seemed more powerful on her than they might be on someone else. In her mellow state of mind, she reached out her hand and he walked over and took it.

"I'm really sorry about all of this," she mumbled, closing her eyes again. "I can't recall ever being in an emergency room for myself. Plenty of times with Harrison. It's probably just a silly little sprain and I'm being a total baby."

Her voice was high pitched as she said, "silly little sprain," and she waved her hand loosely through the air for effect.

She opened her eyes, blinking to focus. "I appreciate you." Her tongue was thicker and she spoke slowly and thoughtfully. "You've been very kind and I am perfectly fine here until the doctor releases me. I know you were packing to head home. You are released from your duties." She patted his hand as tiny tears formed in the corners of her eyes, belying her valiant speech.

Ben leaned over and pushed her hair away from her face, catching a stray tear as it fell. "I will not go anywhere until I'm certain you're safely back in your room looking out at the ocean," he said. "Michael is on his way. He said to tell you he loves you and he will be here as fast as he can."

Alyce remained quiet as her fuzzy brain considered all of this. Sitting in her chair, looking at the ocean sounded divine. That was all she had wanted in the first place. Just to be alone and quiet and embrace life as the single woman she was destined to be.

Yet, she'd only been alone for two days before meeting Ben. He had shown her that being single would not be scary and could include new friends she might never have known. Whatever lay ahead, Alyce was sure she would be fine. Life had been redefined and she was adapting.

She shifted her head on the pillow and said, "Thank you, Ben. For everything. You are a noble man." She closed her eyes and another tear escaped. "I'm glad I got to know you now and not before, when you were that other guy."

Ben smiled and gave her one of his hand hugs. "We likely wouldn't have given each other the time of day. Think of all we would have missed."

Right at that moment the doctor appeared. "Mr. Keriman?" he asked, directed at Ben. Before Ben could speak, Michael rushed in behind them and said, "That would be me. I'm Michael Keriman."

Ben quickly backed away from Alyce's side. "I'm a friend. This is Alyce's husband," he said, gesturing toward Michael. "I'll leave you guys alone."

"Stay," Alyce spoke. "You brought me this far. Doctor?"

"Well," he said, glancing between the two men before directly addressing Alyce. "I am Dr. Dean Henry, and you have a pretty nasty sprain. There's a possible fracture in the bone, but there's too much swelling to tell. I'm sending you home in a boot. However, I would advise you to stay off it completely for the next forty-eight hours. Apply ice packs and take ibuprofen and let's see if we can get that swelling down. Come back in and we'll get a clearer picture. I will give you something for the pain to take as needed. Otherwise," and he glanced between the two men, "keep the excitement to a minimum and no beach volleyball."

He patted Alyce's shoulder and left them there. The three of them. Alyce felt no strong connection to either man. She just really wanted to go to sleep. Michael walked over and, leaning in, gave her a kiss on the forehead. She inhaled his familiar scent, noticing a comfort there. Right then, all she wanted was peace on earth and to be out of that hospital bed.

What a morning it had been! Her stomach growled loudly, reminding her and Ben of their abandoned breakfast.

"Sounds like somebody's hungry," Michael said, and they all laughed.

Ben said, "I think I'll go out to the waiting room. I can drive you guys back to the resort, unless you have your car?"

"No, I don't. That would be great," Michael said as he turned his attention to Alyce.

There was something different in his eyes. Humility? Respect? She was too loopy to sort it out.

"Do you mind if I see your ankle?" he asked tenderly. He raised the sheet covering her legs. Even since coming into the ER the shades of purple and blue had deepened and spread. It was a nasty-looking injury. Michael frowned. "How'd this happen?" he asked.

"Stepped in a hole," Alyce answered matter-of-factly.

Michael seemed content with that answer. "It can happen to the best of us," he said. He gently replaced the sheet, taking extra care around her ankle. As he did so, he asked, "May I please hold you for just a minute?"

Alyce was taken aback by his demeanor. Her bold, assuming husband was sheepishly asking for permission to touch his wife. It was a little disarming, but a wise approach for him to take. He seemed hesitant to do anything within Alyce's personal space without first seeking permission.

Without answering, Alyce sat up slightly and shifted in the bed, making it easier for him to sit beside her. Michael wrapped her in his arms. It was exactly as he had hoped. She still fit perfectly in his embrace. Alyce was aware of Michael's long, audible inhale as he pressed his head against hers. He exhaled—a slow, silent release as he settled himself around her. Comfort. The sanctuary of a familiar place that one never knew they missed until returning. Michael silently vowed that, if it were up to him, he would never be apart from Alyce again.

Chapter Twenty-One

ALYCE AND MICHAEL

*A*lyce sat in her chair by the window, looking into the backyard. It wasn't the same beauty as the beach, but it was still most beautiful to her. Her ankle had begun to heal nicely, although she still wore the clunky boot except to sleep. Thankfully nothing was broken. For now, it was early morning, so she dutifully kept her bare foot and ankle propped on the ottoman before her.

She turned as Michael entered the room, steaming cup of coffee in his hands. "Here you go," he said as he set it on the table beside her.

"Thank you," Alyce said. She picked it up and took a sip. "Mmmm, perfect."

In a second, Michael reappeared with his own cup. He made his way to the end of the sofa closest to her. The end table where he gently sat his mug had transformed into a gathering spot for him. He had accumulated a pair of reading glasses, a couple of highlighters and pens, a journal, and his Bible. He reached for a book there and opened to the day's reading.

After a little time passed he became aware that Alyce was looking at him. When he glanced up, she said, "Share with me?"

Michael read from his book. "To be loved by someone without pause or hesitation, all of our grotesque injuries and filthy wounds, is the greatest and truest and highest gift. But should we be given the opportunity to *extend* such love—therein lies the double blessing. To *extend* great love is to fully comprehend the *gift* of love."

He continued reading, "No one has greater love than this—that one lays down his life for his friends. John 15:13." Michael sat for a minute in silence. He spoke softly, "Alyce, I have never known anything but love from you. I tried to push it aside. It looked like I wanted no more of it, but I knew all along that I hoped it would be waiting when I returned. I was the most selfish human being on the planet. You deserved better, but I'm quite certain you have deserved more from me all along. I am so over myself—my agenda, my needs, my wants. I was completely blind to the fact that what we have built all these years is a full and amazing life. I just hope it's not too late."

"I'm not sure you'll understand this, but a lot of what you're saying to me, I have said recently to the LORD," Alyce said. "I put you and the kids in His place without realizing it. I expected y'all to satisfy my empty spaces and complete me. I've realized that you guys might not always be there, but He will. He wants to fill all my spaces. That means I've always got an abundant supply to spill over onto you. You weren't alone in your misguided affections, Michael. I was there, too."

"I almost choked the life out of our relationship with my expectations and neediness. I would have never in a million years said that a year ago! I'm so not happy with what you did, but I am elated over the catalyst it has been for change in our lives. Michael, I love you, but we've both got to find our sufficiency in God, because we have no promise that we'll be here for each other tomorrow."

Michael appeared poised to protest, so Alyce raised her hand and continued.

"Sickness and aging can change us. Eventually, one of us is going to die. But we both have to recognize God as our source for everything. He gave us each other out of His great love. He will sustain us if ever we can't be here for one another, no matter the cause."

Michael sat staring at his wife. "I sure love you, Alyce Keriman," he said.

"I know, Michael Keriman," she replied. "I wish I'd known before what I know now about myself. I could have helped you, maybe, and not been so needy. I am a very capable daughter of the Creator of the Universe. His sufficiency is boundless. I will never feel unloved again. I love Him so much. He has given me—given *us*—a new chance at life as He intended. But it won't be easy."

"I know," Michael said. "I only pray there comes a day you know you can trust me again."

Alyce had drilled him with questions about his living arrangements—how much money he had blown on the apartment and trips and gifts and all the trappings of his lifestyle. But mostly about the various times when she had confronted him, fully in the right, when he had dismissed her and made her feel ridiculous. Each of those times, he confirmed, he had been lying to her about the affair.

Now she felt at the very least validated. Trust would not be easily regained. There were many questions she would ask and there would be many more moments she would doubt him. It was going to be a tremendous challenge. At times, she would be strong to meet the challenge head-on. Other times, Michael would have to wait for her to process and navigate through them.

"Not to change the subject, but isn't it time for that pastor you like to watch?" Michael hated to interrupt their talk, but the entire day stretched before them. Alyce had not been out except to see the doctor in the two weeks since they'd been home. Likewise, Michael had only left to keep appointments at the office. They needed the time to reconnect and Alyce was desperate for her ankle to heal before Lillian's senior show. She had no desire to be hobbling around in that dratted boot at her daughter's shining moment.

Michael reached for the remote and passed it to Alyce. She turned to the channel as another pastor finished his message. Alyce took out her notebook and Bible, then reached for her coffee and took several sips.

As the program began each week, there would be clips of the key points to come in the message ahead. Alyce listened eagerly and settled into her seat.

"You and I will never walk fully in God's unconditional love until we have been willing to love others as He has—unconditionally."

Another point flashed as the pastor spoke.

"God never said we'd be able to trust one another. He said trust in the LORD. All we can trust is what Jesus says and does in others around us."

That was very familiar. Hadn't Ben quoted something similar to her? She decided to hit the record button. This sermon might take several viewings to process its message entirely.

"One day, I'm gonna stand before the LORD and He's not going to ask me, how well did all these people love *you*, but rather, how well did *you love as Me*?"

Alyce was fully engaged. Her heart tuned in to the next twenty minutes while she scribbled furiously, taking notes on all that was said. She loved studying the Word for herself, but she deeply appreciated a great preacher. One who could explain the Word in a way that was like waving a huge magnifying glass over the ancient script, bringing the details into focus.

For years she had prayed that God would help her understand the Bible. She rationalized that why else would He have written it if it wasn't for everyone to understand and apply to their lives? It had not been easy to stay focused, but she faithfully went back day after day. Now every morning she had to peel herself away from her Bible study.

Time in the Word educated Alyce about God's character. She was convinced that He was incapable of lying. Lying would violate His very nature. He was truth. She also knew that His Word sometimes asked difficult things of His children so that He could prove Himself strong in their lives. But He promised to always be faithful.

Alyce recalled the words of a dear friend who had been a pastor to them in their early-married years. One of her favorite quotes he used was, "I can't; God never said I could. He can, and He always said He would!" Later, Alyce looked it up and found that it was originally attributed to Major Ian Thomas. Whoever said it, it was a truth she needed now.

Sitting in her chair as the sermon ended, Alyce was overwhelmed by the enormity of a reconciliation. She wanted the two of them to overcome, but she knew not one soul who had ever attempted it, let alone succeeded. She shifted toward Michael and turned off the television.

"I am committed to you and to this marriage. I love you and I want us to be together, but I have to know you are in it for the long haul. I don't want to be a statistic. I want to be the little old couple holding hands in the nursing home. I want to take our grandkids on trips together, just like we planned. I want to know that you are pursuing a relationship with God as fervently as you are pursuing a relationship with me. I *know* our relationships with God won't look the same, but I have to know that you are in tune with what He's working on for your life. If we are both focused on the same goal of knowing Him fully, He will make it work—somehow, some way—He will do it. But we will have to stay close to Him."

Michael was by her chair on one knee in a flash. He took her hands in his and said, "I promise! Please don't kick me to the curb. I know you're scared. Quite honestly, I'm unsure of all that's going on inside of me right now. But there is not another person on the planet that I believe I can be fully myself with—who believes for the best in my life—as you."

Alyce did something she'd never done before. She bowed her head and began praying for them. "Father, we are messed up. We are broken. Our brains are scattered in confusion with all that has transpired these past two weeks, much less the past year. But You are not the author of confusion. You said You would make crooked paths straight and that You would shine a light on the way with Your Word. I am so thankful that You have never left our sides, even as we have been apart. I thank You for my husband and I ask You to bless him and guard his heart and mind as he seeks to follow the well-lit path You have for him. Help us, LORD, because right now we feel feeble. Make us strong in Your power and Your truth. Amen."

Michael was weeping. Alyce was not accustomed to so much emotion from him. He laid his head in her lap and she stroked his hair as he cried. When he lifted it, Alyce looked into his eyes and felt she was really seeing the true Michael for the very first time.

He got up from the floor and grabbed his coffee cup. "All this revelation has made me hungry. I'm going to fix us some brunch. Does an omelet sound good?"

"Sounds delicious," Alyce responded, grateful for some alone time to process emotions. She was happy for her husband, but she was not ready to let it all go. Deep down, she felt certain that it would happen, but Michael would have to extend a lot of grace as she worked her way through things she'd been suppressing.

On the drive home from the beach, she had spoken honestly with him about her feelings. "You feel joyful and lighthearted because you are free from the bondage that guilt and lies can clamp on us. You don't have to carry that burden now. But I am just beginning to come to terms with many things that you have done. I don't honestly understand *why* you did them. I need time. *I* want to feel lighthearted again. I need understanding. I'm not sure you've got enough to give me."

Alyce remembered another quote by Sir Ian Thomas she'd discovered when doing research about him. She'd written it in the back of her Bible. Flipping there she read these words:

"The Lord seemed to make plain to me that night, through my tears of bitterness: 'You see, for seven years, with utmost sincerity, you have been trying to live for Me, on My behalf, the life that I have been waiting for seven years to live through you.' That night, all in the space of an hour, Ian Thomas discovered the secret of the adventurous life. He said: 'I got up the next morning to an entirely different Christian life, but I want to emphasize this: I had not received one iota more than I had already had for seven years!' "

Alyce closed her Bible and silently breathed a prayer, "Father, I need Your power and grace to live one day at a time. But I thank You for the gift of the Holy Spirit who can do things through me that I can never accomplish, as I surrender everything to You. I want You to live the life through me that I have been trying to live without You. LORD, will You please put Your hand over my mouth when I need to be silent, and will You speak up when I need to be bold? I confess I am exhausted. I can't, but You can and You said You always will."

Chapter Twenty-Two

ALYCE AND MICHAEL

*A*lyce was exuberant for many reasons. They had been home for six weeks and she and Michael were enjoying each other like never before. She once again had joy from the little things with him. Things she had missed or perhaps even overlooked.

They celebrated Michael's birthday with a small party of family and friends at their favorite Mexican restaurant. When they arrived home, Alyce allowed Michael to sleep in their bed for the first time since he'd come back. He had been sleeping in Maggie's old room, even in the mess it was, while they began intense counseling and sorted through their issues together. They were not intimate yet, but Alyce allowed Michael to cuddle with her as they drifted off to sleep.

Another reason for Alyce's exuberance was the slightly bulging tummy of her older daughter. A baby was coming, and who didn't love a baby? The thought of being a grandmother was thrilling. Alyce confessed she spent too much time agonizing over what the baby should call her. The distraction was frivolous and fun, two words she realized she'd missed in her life.

There was the matter of Michael's apartment to disperse. Alyce's practical side would have helped box and sort and give things away. It would not have been in her best interest, nor would it have been good for their reconciliation. It proved a blessing that she had been instructed to stay off her foot.

Michael had invited Carrie and her husband to come to the apartment and see if they might use any of his furniture. They took many things. Carrie was giddy over the opportunity to add quality pieces to their ragtag collection of flea market finds and hand-me-downs. The rest of Michael's things were donated. He wanted to be done with the entire process as quickly as possible.

There was work still going on at the house, but Alyce was more determined to complete it in a timely manner. Maggie would need her when the baby arrived. Michael was fully engaged in the entire remodel and had added his own ideas to hers. Now that their budget included his salary, things would be more manageable.

Life had been pretty sweet around the Keriman household. There was one potentially rough patch the day that Michael made a trip to the extra garage for some tools. Alyce had been surprised that Michael never questioned where she'd gotten the money for her little beach vacation and the renovations she'd completed. In the midst of all the reconciling, perhaps he'd decided to save that for a later date.

Which was fine until the morning at breakfast when he said, "I feel like I want to get my hands dirty. I think I can do the work of tearing out the tile in the guest bathroom. I've watched them do it on TV and it sure looks like fun. I think I'll head out to the barn and grab a crowbar and mallet. Maybe even a sledgehammer. What do you think?"

Alyce had nearly choked on her oatmeal. She did not want Michael anywhere near the shed. "Are you sure that's a good idea? I mean, we are paying the contractors to do it all. Maybe you should leave that work to them."

Michael stood up with his empty bowl, walked over, and began rinsing it in the sink. As he dried his hands on a dish towel he said, "Nah! I can do it! Besides, I think it'll be a little therapeutic to bust out some of the old to see it replaced with the new."

Alyce mustered her best nonchalant performance.

"I'm happy to get the tools for you." She was careful to avoid eye contact as she picked up her bowl and empty juice glass. But Michael was already headed to the door. He glanced back over his shoulder with a look that said, *What is the matter with you?*

Alyce busied herself with emptying the dishwasher so she could load their breakfast dishes. He was back in a jiffy with the necessary tools. She steeled herself for his explosion, but he walked in the door and headed straight to the guest bath. Alyce froze on the spot. She heard him coming back down the hallway and again prepared herself for the onslaught. Nothing.

"Forgot to get work gloves!" he said cheerily as he headed out again. Alyce smiled weakly. Surely she couldn't escape twice. But sure enough, Michael came back in, waving his gloves and whistling a happy tune.

When the coast was clear, Alyce herself headed out to the garage. Opening the door, she half expected to see it, but no, the Jeep was definitely gone. How could he have missed that it wasn't there?

Aside from their two trips to the beach and the occasional jaunt to the store, Michael never drove the Jeep. The weather had to be just right and he had to be in the mood to fool with the top. However he wanted to play with his toy, Alyce felt he deserved a little diversion in his life. Plus, there was always the promise of "one day," where she imagined the two of them heading out on adventures together.

It was a particularly rough day a few months back, when she'd encountered more details of her husband's indiscretions. Squirrels had gotten into the attic and one of Jackson's friends had come to help patch their access hole. This required tools and a ladder. She sent him to the shed for supplies and he returned drooling over the Jeep. He wanted to know how much she'd take for it. Alyce had very few mean bones in her body, but timing was everything.

At first, she'd told him it wasn't for sale, but after seeing the charges added to their card by Michael, she'd done her research and come up with a price. He bought it. And before she could talk herself out of it, Alyce paid for her vacation. And called the carpenter to get started on her bathroom.

Now, walking back inside, she wondered what to do about the entire situation. The Jeep was gone. That was a fact. But what about when Michael noticed it was missing? Should she wait for that revelation or come clean on her own?

She felt her pride rising, ready to defend her actions against his long list of crimes. Would he seriously have the nerve to get angry with her after all he'd done? She was feisty before she made it back to the house and ready for him to dare ask her about the Jeep. If he said a word she would let him have it.

But he didn't ask. And she didn't offer. By the time they got in bed that night, she had cooled down, the guest bathroom had been demolished, and the mess cleaned up. Now they both lay on their backs in the dark. Without realizing it, Alyce let out a huge sigh, which signaled to Michael that she was awake.

"Did you get a good price for it?" he voiced into the darkness. Was he talking about the Jeep? Alyce held her breath and wondered if she should feign sleep. Or perhaps play dumb?

"A good price for what?" she asked, not willing to hang herself unnecessarily.

"For the Jeep. I've known that it's gone for about a week now."

What? Alyce hesitated. She decided on the path of least resistance. "Enough for a really nice vacation."

"I'm glad," Michael said, turned on his side to face her, and kissed her on the head. "Sweet dreams, baby. I love you."

"I love you, too," she replied.

Chapter Twenty-Three
LILLIAN'S ART SHOW

*C*risis averted. And without any bloodshed. In years to come, they would laugh every time Michael headed to the garage. "Anything I need to know?" he would ask.

So much between them had changed. They had experienced miracle after miracle. Tonight would be the culmination of a much-anticipated year of work on the part of their middle child. She had not shared much about the exhibit. Lillian held things closely that way.

As they drove past the plate-glass windows of the refurbished storefront where the artists displayed their work, a light, misty rain was falling. Alyce prayed the weather wouldn't hinder folks from venturing out. She was not disappointed. Strings of white lights glowed from inside, sending a welcoming beacon into the darkness. The scene through the windows seemed a work of art in itself, with the many beautiful people milling about. It was a picture of laughter and merriment.

Michael let her out, then left to park the car. She scooted inside, thankful to be rid of the boot, but attentive to step carefully even so. Gleaming wood floors and old brick walls were the perfect background to showcase the art. Alyce stood gazing, overwhelmed by the sea of people. An underclassman greeted her and offered a program describing the flow and theme for the works presented.

"Tonight's artist is Lillian Marie Keriman. She is a senior fine arts major who plans to continue her education in hopes of working with autistic children. All projects are for sale after the show, with the exception of the final piece in the exhibit. Please enjoy a beverage as you immerse yourself in the artistry that is Lillian."

Alyce allowed the young lady to finish her talk before confiding in her that Lillian was her own dear girl. "I just loved hearing what you had to say," she said with a wink.

She turned to walk away, but the girl stepped closer and said, "It is nice to meet you! You should know that Lillian is one of my mentors. I do so love the heart of her work."

Alyce thanked her, soft tears glistening in her eyes. These were the moments she held closely when she felt that reconciling her marriage was going to demand too much. She knew deep down that there wasn't another human on the planet who shared her history and would also share her enthusiasm for all that would transpire with their children. Anything was possible and this Alyce knew well. She had to choose joy, even in heartbreaking circumstances. She had to choose love, even when she couldn't feel it.

She moved deeper into the crowd, looking for familiar faces. Michael came through the door, stamping his feet and shaking an umbrella behind him. She loved that her heart thrilled once again when she saw him. He was a good-looking man. Perhaps it was just in her eyes, though hers were all that mattered. His once-dark hair was in fierce competition with the gray, but it only enhanced his appearance. She watched as the young student handed him a program and they engaged in conversation. The entire time his brown eyes scanned the room.

Catching her gaze, those eyes lit up like she never again thought they would. He strode across the floor and leaned in to kiss her on the cheek. "You look amazing," he whispered in her ear and she felt a warm glow spread across her cheeks. She almost said, "You say that to all the girls," but stopped herself. Some things she would never be able to say again. But she would not allow her thoughts to change the effervescent mood of this magical evening.

Lillian saw the two of them and made a beeline to their side. "Where have you guys been? I've been waiting for you to do an official presentation of the show."

Michael and Alyce looked at each other quizzically, then followed her to an area near the front of the massive room. Maggie and Jackson appeared, as well as Harrison, looking dapper in a navy blazer and striped bow tie. Lillian held a glass of champagne and tapped on its side with the back of her ring to get everyone's attention.

"I'd like to thank you all for coming out tonight and braving the rain. This project has been one of the greatest experiences of my life. It has been hard. It has been exhilarating. It has taken several twists and turns. At one point, I thought it was doomed, but I decided to keep at it despite all that seemed to be set against it."

She looked at her parents with tears in her eyes. They were both confused by such emotion from their normally thick-skinned girl. Undeterred, Lillian continued.

"I arrived at the idea sitting in my philosophy class last spring. Professor Lewis posed the question, 'What is love?' I carried that question with me long after the class discussion had ended. Its implications went deep inside of me, because I'm a person of faith in Jesus Christ. So, what does love look like in light of who I say I am as a child of God?"

Lillian had everyone's attention. She drew in a shaky breath and forged ahead. "My personal reference for love to this point has come through my family and how they have loved. Me. Each other. And, most importantly, how my parents have patterned love in my life. Many of you know the words I am about to share, but some of you don't know they come from the Bible. Love is patient and kind. It is not envious. Love does not brag; it is not puffed up. It is not rude; it is not self-serving; it is not easily angered or resentful. It is not glad about injustice, but rejoices in the truth. All of these qualities I have experienced firsthand through the love of my family."

She paused as the crowd responded with light applause.

"So, what is love? Based on these attributes, I have come to the conclusion that love is selfless; love serves. That means it is always outwardly focused. As you walk through the exhibit," Lillian gestured toward the first group of photography, "my desire is to portray love as it was displayed by the One whom I believe loves us in the truest form of the word. I realized that a lot of times He was feeding folks and giving them drink. I think that showed His concern for their physical needs while teaching them about His Father, God. You will see art that depicts His first act of service, which was to turn water into wine at a wedding in Canaan. There will also be the feeding of five thousand people with a small boy's lunch of five loaves of bread and two fish.

"As you embrace the elements of my exhibit, you will see I showcase the love between my parents with pictures I took nearly two years ago at the celebration of their twenty-fifth wedding anniversary. Tonight is their first time seeing them. Their love is miraculous. Many people may say that about a marriage, but I am honored to have personally witnessed this miracle. Their love is a perfect example of the next part of that passage on love from the Bible. Love bears all things, believes all things, hopes all things, endures all things. My mom and dad are trophies of grace. They have patterned for me and my siblings what servant love looks like as they have loved each other."

"And, finally, there is the element of Christ's sacrificial service, even as His death loomed in front of Him. He didn't retreat into His agony. He found His friends and He fellowshipped. He washed feet. He broke bread and poured wine. He served. He gave sacrificially with absolutely no concern for His own comfort and without fear of what He knew was to come. He wants us to love each other in that same manner.

"Not all of us have been the recipient of sacrificial love, but we can be. And more importantly, we can love sacrificially, which is the greatest gift of service. But it is only in receiving what He offers that we are able to give. We can only give out of His abundance. Jesus is love."

Lillian raised her glass in the air. "I would like to dedicate my senior art show to my parents, Alyce and Michael Keriman, for their unwavering commitment to love well, no matter the cost. No one has greater love than this—that one lays down his life for his friends. The two of you have given me so much. I thank God for your example in my life—sometimes of what not to do," she said with a little laugh, "but mostly what I should do to express true love. Salùte!"

On cue, everyone raised a glass and Michael took advantage of that moment to lean over and give Alyce a big kiss. The crowd erupted into cheers and applause.

Alyce was captivated by her daughter's creativity. She followed the sound of water as the first of the exhibit unfolded. Along the way were various-sized photos of people serving food and drink. Alyce's favorite was of a beautiful outdoor feast with the sun setting in the hills behind. Lillian had timed the photo so that the loaded table appeared to extend into the sun's brilliant splendor.

Or perhaps her favorite was of an old woman proudly hugging a huge bowl of pasta, extended as if offering a helping for yourself. Alyce was intrigued that Lillian captured every wrinkle of her face, each line traceable to the joy in her eyes. Her gray hair was pulled back in a bun. Little, wispy coils sprang out all around, hinting at her just-completed work in the kitchen. The vibrant colors of her clothing and surroundings indicated this was a woman of vim and vigor.

A vivid picture of a large, earthen vessel of water was mounted high. Weathered hands tilted the jar, as what appeared to be the last few drops of water poured out. Several smaller pictures cascaded down from that one and in each was a single droplet caught in midair. Lillian had colored the photos to depict the transition from water to wine. With each photo the saturation of red intensified. The last one was a rich crimson color. At the bottom was the actual vessel from the first picture full of a crimson liquid to represent the wine.

Next, Lillian displayed gorgeous pictures of the seashore, a fish market, and a most interesting throng of young people, each one lifting a small loaf above their head.

"How did you accomplish that?" Alyce asked.

Lillian explained how, with the help of friends, she'd gone to Bonnaroo, a music festival outside of Nashville, and recruited a crowd to participate in the photo. "That was a pretty tough picture to coordinate, but they got to keep the bread!" she laughed.

Alyce became aware of music in the background. It was a song her daddy used to sing as he played with the grandkids in the yard. She had no idea that Lillian remembered this song, much less had paid attention to its message. Johnny Cash crooned very subtly in the background, "In the little Canaan town the word went all around." She caught snippets of the words. Each one captured an element of the display—"He turned the water into wine," and "with a little fish and bread, they said every one was fed." Lillian had incorporated the song to engage multiple senses in her art immersion. There was even the fragrance of fresh-baked bread, a feat Alyce would have to explore later. Her girl was surrounded by new enthusiasts and this was her moment.

She passed through an archway of grapevines intertwined with Rose of Sharon, a transition to the next display. A calligraphy scroll bore the scripture from Song of Solomon, chapter 2:

I am the spring crocus blooming on the Sharon Plain,
the lily of the valley.
Like a lily among thistles
is my darling among young women.
Like the finest apple tree in the orchard
is my lover among other young men.
I sit in his delightful shade
and taste his delicious fruit.
He escorts me to the banquet hall;
it's obvious how much he loves me.

Here Alyce encountered pictures from their anniversary party. When Lillian had described this portion, Alyce was uncertain as to how it would fit into the progression that otherwise dealt with Christ's sacrificial love. But the segue seemed natural as she observed the pictures, none of which exposed their faces. There were close-ups of their interlocked hands as Michael escorted her onto the dance floor. Michael helping her with her chair. Her ear and his mouth as he whispered something just between the two of them. Her hands straightening his tie. And finally, the two of them from behind, sitting on a bench outside the venue, Alyce's head leaned over on Michael's shoulder. Each photo bore a caption. "Believes all things." "Hopes all things." "Bears all things." "Endures all things." "Love never fails."

Moving on, there was a hand-woven cloth that Lillian had made, simple, but with beautiful craftsmanship. Next to it sat a basin of water.

An earthenware plate and cup that Lillian had made completed the display. Alyce recognized their significance as they represented the Last Supper in the upper room where Christ used a cloth to wash His friends' feet before serving them the meal that would be repeated throughout the centuries as Christians observed the sacrament.

And finally, the culmination of Lillian's show. Alyce rounded the corner and her breath caught in her throat. Before her was the most beautiful cross she had ever seen. It had been carved from maple and polished to a brilliant sheen. No wonder she had seen little of Lillian in the past year. She had tackled some monumental tasks!

The placard attached simply stated: THIS IS LOVE. Beside it, crafted in beautiful freestyle script that was an art piece itself, hung the Prayer of St. Francis painted on burlap:

Lord, make me an instrument of thy peace.
Where there is hatred, let me sow love;
Where there is injury, pardon;
Where there is doubt, faith;
Where there is despair, hope;
Where there is darkness, light;
Where there is sadness, joy.
O divine Master, grant that I may not so much seek
To be consoled as to console,
To be understood as to understand,
To be loved as to love;
For it is in giving that we receive;
It is in pardoning that we are pardoned;
It is in dying to self that we are born to eternal life.

"What do you think, Mama?"

Lillian sidled up beside Alyce and took her hand, intertwining their fingers just like when she was a little girl. She leaned her head on Alyce's shoulder and looked over at her daddy. "This is my favorite."

Michael was overwhelmed with emotion. To think of where he was only two months ago. His mind would not let him forget the pain he'd inflicted by the callousness of his heart. And all the while, his daughter was believing for her parents, the center of her senior exhibit. He wasn't sure what she would have done had he not come to his senses and returned to be restored to his place beside his wife.

He stood looking at the cross and felt the forgiveness of his Father. He knew it was a long road ahead of him. He had a lot to overcome, but what was that verse? "I have overcome the world." Michael knew he would not walk alone. Another verse came to his mind, "I do not consider myself to have attained this. Instead I am single-minded: Forgetting the things that are behind and reaching out for the things that are ahead, with this goal in mind, I strive toward the prize of the upward call of God in Christ Jesus."

Lillian stepped between her parents and the cross and addressed the small crowd around them. "I believe there is one more surprise here for someone." Michael cleared his throat and regained his composure. He stepped up beside Lillian.

"Hi, everyone," he said loudly. Michael waited until he had their attention. "I'm Michael Keriman and this talented young lady is my daughter," he said as he put his arm around her shoulders and squeezed tightly. "Recently I have experienced the sacrificial love of someone out of the ordinary. He offered me the gift of friendship when I least deserved it and would not have expected a thing from him, because he was a total stranger. Today, I am happy to count him as one of the truest friends I've ever known."

Michael continued, "About two months ago, I visited Lillian in her studio and caught a hint of what this evening would encompass. A few days ago, I asked if I might invite my new friend here to thank him in front of all of you, to which she willingly agreed."

Michael looked at his daughter, overcome with emotion. Lillian took his cue and continued, "Of course I agreed! What better way to end this experience of sacrificial love than art in real life? Ben, will you come out here?"

Alyce was stunned. She had not had any contact with Ben since he dropped them at the resort from the ER. Now, he came through the doorway carrying a lovely bouquet of purple irises. He handed them to Lillian and congratulated her on her show. He walked over to Alyce with that familiar sparkle. "Well, hello," he said as he gave her a brotherly hug. Alyce gave Michael an incredulous look.

"Surprised?" Michael asked.

"That's putting it mildly," Alyce responded. "What in the world?"

Michael came up and put a protective arm around Alyce's waist. "Ben has kept in touch with me since the beach. He wanted, of course, to make sure you were okay, but he has also agreed to come alongside me as an accountability partner of sorts."

"But mostly just a friend," Ben interjected shyly. "I have felt this was my calling. I never dreamed it would happen in this manner, but, hey, God can do whatever He wants, right?"

Alyce was so confounded that she could only stand there, taking it all in. "You must be Maggie," Ben said, "I recognize a little mother when I see one. And you're Jackson?"

The kids had quizzical looks on their faces. Harrison stepped forward of his own accord and said, "Hello, sir. I'm Harrison Keriman," shaking Ben's hand vigorously as he did so.

Michael stepped in. "And you met Lillian, the star of this little soiree. I appreciate your coming all this way, Ben. Your investment in our family has meant so much. I know that what you've learned about love came at a great sacrifice to you. I appreciate your willingness to share it with me. I am grateful and honored to call you friend."

Alyce still could not find words. How could she explain what Ben had done for her to her children? She could not, and it wasn't necessary. All that mattered was that she knew deep in her heart she was better and different because of his friendship. She knew that she owed him a tremendous debt of gratitude. She was thankful that she had not seen the last of him, because his love for the Lord would be a great encouragement to Michael. She breathed a prayer of thanksgiving that God had spared their time at the beach from taking a different direction. That He had taken an abundance of heartache between three individuals and rewritten the story—forgiven and forgiving.

Alyce reached over and took Michael by the hand. She suddenly realized that her little brood was gathered at the foot of the cross. Should she point that out? No. Somehow, she knew that was meant just for her. The foot of the cross was where they all needed to stay. And when more difficult days arose, it was there she wanted to return with her clan, time after time. Her role was to love them well by covering them in prayer.

Harrison slipped over to his mom and gave her a bear hug. "Love is really nice, isn't it, Mom?" he asked.

"Yes it is, baby, when you finally see it for what it truly is."

ABOUT THE AUTHOR

 **Tonda B Solomon** met her husband in college. After he completed his law degree they moved back to his small town and began their fairytale. Four sons, a home in the country, a good name in the community…then came the affair and the almost certain destruction of their Camelot.

A bold decision to relocate to Tennessee proved wisest for their marriage. Over fifteen years later they have learned much about themselves as the LORD has quieted the fears of the past. Many pivotal trials have impacted their lives. They have no doubt that they are better together.

Tonda's characters illustrate universal truths she has gleaned as the path of her life has led full circle to a quiet contentment and knowing. There is no doubt that three things remain: faith, hope, and love…and the greatest of these truly is love, freely given and freely received.

A voracious appetite for reading, traveling, music of all sorts, and experiencing the world through her favorite littles (she doesn't feel old enough for the "grand" word) fills her days. She and her husband are now empty nesters (with a not-so-empty nest) who reside in Franklin, Tennessee.

CPSIA information can be obtained
at www.ICGtesting.com
Printed in the USA
BVHW030841040220
571380BV00001B/93